# Golden Buttons

A VICKY LORING STORY

# Golden Buttons

by Wynn Kincade
illustrated by
Charles Burger

Golden Press
New York

# Contents

# 1

## Eastward, Ho!

A GENIE with a shock of white hair and a stern look swirled out of the lamp. Magically, a brilliant green typewriter floated toward him. As he pounded rapidly at the keys, he chanted a brisk song. "Assemble all the known facts. Keep your eyes open and get facts, facts, facts." The genie's voice rose in a spiraling echo, then suddenly died away.

Vicky Loring stirred in her sleep. Where did she get Aladdin's lamp? Who was this strangely familiar genie? The stern face loomed before her again. Of course, of course. The genie was Uncle Matt! She'd better answer him.

"Yes, Uncle Matt. Oh, I *will* get all the facts," Vicky called anxiously after the ghostly figure as it faded away.

Vicky Loring's head came off the pillow as though pulled by strings. She blinked her eyes rapidly and pushed the disheveled curls from her forehead.

A quick glance about her brought her from the fantasy of her Arabian Nights dream to the reality of here and now. She knew where she was—and why. She was on a transoceanic jet, high above the Atlantic Ocean, shooting comfortably toward the little-known, exotic, oil-rich land of Zourab. This was only the beginning of the fascinating trip. She'd be landing soon for a brief stop in Paris, or rather, at the airport at Orly, some fifteen miles outside the city.

Vicky stretched lazily and arched her shoulders to unwind the kinks. "No wonder I dreamed I was a female Aladdin," she said half-aloud. "This trip is almost as unbelievable as a magic carpet ride."

Everything she had read about the land of Zourab had reminded her of the *Thousand and One Nights*. And small wonder the genie looked like Uncle Matt. Uncle Matt had urged her to find out all she could about this tiny spot on the map of the Middle East.

She chuckled as she thought of how amused her "Uncle" Matt would be when she described her dream to him. "Really," she would write him, "you made a very handsome genie and sounded exactly like your grumpy self."

"Uncle" Matt Matson had been Vicky's boss until a few short weeks before. He was head of the news bureau of the Continental Broadcasting Company, and her adopted uncle. Her father's best friend, Matt Matson had known Vicky since her babyhood. His fondness for Vicky could never be completely hidden in spite of his attempts to cover it with gruffness, especially when he was guiding her in her job.

A muted snore escaped from Vicky's seat companion, her father. She nudged him gently. He shifted his position and settled back into soundless sleep.

"Well," the girl thought. "So this is the gentleman who said he'd wake *me* in time to see the first European landfall. Humph. He'll sleep smack into Orly if I let him."

She gazed fondly at the lean, tanned face of her father. Even in sleep, Kenneth Loring looked like the active, alive person he was. Seated now with his arms folded, his handsome head thrown back, he did not seem to be asleep, but busily gathering his thoughts as he did before asking a piercing question of some world-famous person during a television interview.

As Vicky watched, she saw a frown crease her father's forehead. "Something's worrying him. Has it anything to do with this assignment in Zourab?" The thought winged through her mind and was quickly gone. And so was the frown on her father's face.

"I'm mighty proud of you, Boss," Vicky murmured into his unhearing ear. Recently, Vicky had been promoted from a "cub" writer at CBC to the job of assistant to her father.

Kenneth Loring was *the* newsman of the Continental Broadcasting Company. Much of what he knew about newsgathering had been taught him by Matt Matson, a newspaper man, but Ken Loring had carved out his own unique career in television. Always hunting for unusual subjects for his famous documentary presentations, he was ready to go anywhere the news took him.

As her father's assistant, Vicky would now travel with him whenever possible. "You're my extra pair of eyes and ears," he explained to her. Her job was to research for facts, to discover interesting details, to keep her eyes open for extraordinary camera effects.

Vicky rummaged for the canvas flight bag she had carried aboard the plane and reached for the shoes she had kicked off. She decided to freshen up and greet her father with a bright-morning face before she started to tease him about oversleeping.

Quietly, Vicky removed the blanket she had thrown over her knees, eased herself out of the seat, and stepped over her father's outstretched legs. Carrying her shoes, she slipped down the aisle of the plane past the still-sleeping passengers.

In the cramped wash-room, Vicky examined herself carefully in the mirror. "Yikes! Look at my hair," she said as she reached for the comb. Quickly she drew it through her dark brown curls. The curls swiftly assumed their usual neat but casual look. Cold water dashed on her face swept the sleepy look from her wide, brown eyes. Vicky next examined the dash of freckles which dotted her tip-tilted nose, then covered them with powder.

"I suppose I'll have a million of them after one day in sun-baked Zourab," she sighed. "Freckles . . . ugh!" She made a face at herself in the mirror.

She could almost hear her Aunt Ellen's voice saying, "That will be enough of that, young lady. It was the good Lord's intention for you to have freckles."

Vicky rubbed the excess make-up from her nose automatically. There, perhaps Aunt Ellen would approve now. Aunt Ellen was Ken Loring's elder sister. She had taken the place of the mother Vicky had never known. Aunt Ellen, in spite of long years spent in New York City, Vicky's home town, lived firmly by the rules learned long ago in her New England girlhood. But beneath her no-nonsense manner was a warm heart and a whimsical sense of humor.

Vicky blew a kiss in the general direction of New York and hoped it would reach Aunt Ellen's cheek.

Morning was seeping into the plane as Vicky walked back to her seat. Somewhere, she could hear the tiny whimper of a hungry baby. A stewardess passed by, holding a wrapped nursing bottle. Vicky could hear the swishing sound of half-smothered yawns from some of the passengers. Arms waved over the backs of seats as passengers stretched from their short rest.

The plane had left Idlewild airport in New York at 8:30 at night and had raced toward daylight. It would land in France at 8:30 in the morning, Paris time. The five-hour difference in time meant an abbreviated night.

Vicky glanced at her watch, still set at New York time. 1:30 A.M. Yet, here was dawn breaking over the Atlantic. She asked the returning stewardess the Paris time and set her watch ahead.

Ken Loring was still sleeping when Vicky reached her seat. Resuming her place near the window, she gazed out, eager to catch her first glimpse of land. She should soon be seeing the coast of France. There! She could just see a dark smudge on the horizon.

Vicky pushed her father's shoulder. "Mr. Loring," she said, "how about showing me the sights of Europe?"

"Wha—what?" Ken Loring jumped at the girl's touch. "Oh, are you awake?" he asked.

"You almost sound disappointed," Vicky answered. "Good thing I was, or I'd have missed my first glimpse of *La Belle France*. Fine alarm clock you turned out to be," she chided with a laugh.

"Oh, well," her father said, yawning, "*La Belle France* hasn't taken the curlers out of her hair yet. She'll have all her make-up on by the time we land. She'll look even better then. Besides," he argued, "you've been in France before."

"But I don't remember much about it. I was too small that time Aunt Ellen and I were there with you."

"Well, you still managed to learn the language. Enough to give you a good start with school French," Ken said.

"I'm still a little nervous about using it, Dad," Vicky confessed. "My school French was pretty rusty until I took those conversational brush-up courses Uncle Matt suggested."

"You'll be back in the swing of it in no time. And you'll need it soon—and from then on. Zourab, you know, was a French protectorate long ago, so most of the natives speak a French 'patois,' a dialect, as well as Arabic."

"I realize that. So I'll just have to wade in and let my irregular verbs fall where they may. I hope they don't injure anybody," she joked.

"That's the spirit." Her father patted her knee. "I think I'd better freshen up for landing. I'll go get ready."

In her father's absence, Vicky began to think of the day ahead of her. They would land at Orly but probably would not go into Paris. Father had mentioned they wouldn't have too much time—just enough for him to make a few calls.

"Perhaps I can telephone Jeff," she mused. "Too bad I won't be able to see his face when I rub *this* trip in." Jeff had been so smug about his Paris assignment. Her thoughts turned toward Paris and Jeff Hubbell.

Jeff Hubbell was a young reporter for World-Wide News, a news service with offices all over the world. Jeff had wangled and maneuvered for a transfer to a European office of World-Wide. In spite of the fact that he was fairly new to journalism, he had succeeded, although Vicky had predicted he wouldn't. Perhaps it was because she really hadn't wanted him to go so far away.

In New York, sometimes digging out the same

stories, they had been rivals, friendly and not-so-friendly. She'd missed seeing him around and she'd missed even more the dates they had had. One thing she hadn't missed at all—his poking fun at her talents as a full-fledged reporter. He'd been positively pompous about his new job abroad, even though it was a temporary spot for him.

"I wonder if he's found someone else to tease and pick on," she thought. A female someone? She dismissed the thought hurriedly. Her father, and their breakfast trays, appeared before more memories of Jeff Hubbell flashed through her mind.

As the plane began its descent, Vicky and her father talked business. As they reviewed the plans made in New York for their stay in Zourab, Vicky realized how many gaps there were in her knowledge of the political situation in this strange country. She knew that the land was ruled by a sort of shah, El Mohama Shah-ja, but that many tribes within the tiny country had jurisdiction over special sections. They were loyal to El Mohama, however, who was educated, modern in his ideas, quite democratic in principle, and loved by his people. But this was the extent of her knowledge, and she hoped to be brought up to date once they got to Zourab.

When the trays had been cleared away, a click from

the plane's loudspeaker alerted Vicky and her father. In French, the stewardess announced the local time and weather conditions, the time of touchdown at Orly, and information about customs and transport into Paris, ending with a polite "*Merci*" for having traveled on the airline. The message was repeated in English.

"I just gave myself a B-plus," Vicky said to her father. "I got most of the French announcement."

Outside the window the sprawling suburbs of Paris, still softly covered with morning haze, tilted slowly past as the plane entered the Orly landing approach pattern.

Like every large air terminal, Orly was bustling with passengers, airline officials, and ground crews. Vicky and her father joined the flow of passengers toward the customs counter where the polite inspectors passed them through quickly.

"Well, that was easy," Vicky remarked to her father as they moved away. "I had visions of eight suspicious officials examining my flight bag with magnifying glasses. They simply asked me if I had any chocolate or cigarettes to declare."

"That's a standard question in most European airports," her father explained.

The two headed for the terminal waiting room. Vicky, in a bright red suit with a short, button-up jacket over a pleated skirt, was glad she had worn flats. In heels she never could keep up with her father's long strides.

Suddenly, she was aware that someone had stepped to her side and was marching along with her. "*Mademoiselle, avez-vous du chocolat ou des cigarettes, ou peut-être, un baiser pour un vieil ami?*" a voice said in awful French with a terrible American accent. The voice was very close.

Vicky braked to a quick stop. She'd know that voice in any language. Jeff Hubbell—and apparently Paris hadn't changed him in the least!

"No chocolate, no cigarettes, and absolutely . . ." she began.

"Don't tell me; let me guess. 'No kiss for an old friend,'" Jeff finished. "Not even a *petit* one?" he pleaded.

Vicky looked up at the blond young man with the short-cropped hair. She stretched as tall as she could on tiptoe and planted a light kiss on his chin. In her flat heels, she just about reached it.

"I'm sort of glad to see you," she said.

"Hi," he said, a wide grin crinkling his face. "Long time no see and *très bon* it is to set eyes upon you."

"Dad, here's Jeff," Vicky called after her father, who, intent upon his next duties, had gone on ahead.

Ken Loring turned. "Glad you came out to say hello, Jeff. I was about to treat Vicky to her first taste of a real French *croissant* in a long time. Perhaps you can do the honors while I make a few phone calls."

"Actually, sir, I came on out to see if I could get a story from you on your Zourab assignment. Any chance?" the young man asked, not even looking at Ken Loring but keeping his gaze fixed on Vicky's fresh face.

"Yes, I'll *bet* you did," Ken said, noticing the direction of Jeff's gaze. "But no, no interview on the way out there. Perhaps when I come back . . ."

Ken Loring broke off and turned his head swiftly toward one of the doors. Vicky saw what had caught his attention. A small, swarthy man, dressed in an ordinary dark suit, but wearing a white headdress topped with two thick black cords, was hurrying in their direction. As the man came nearer, Vicky recognized the odd headgear with the two dangling white pieces which hung down on each side of the man's deeply tanned face. "A *kaffiyeh*," she thought to herself. "That's what the men in Zourab wear."

"Monsieur Loring?" the man said, solemnly bending his head in a stately bow. At the same time, he held a white envelope toward Vicky's father. Without another word, he bowed again and sidled away, vanishing in the crowd.

Ken Loring broke the wide, emerald-green wax seal on the envelope, removed the thick white folded paper inside, and read hastily. Finally, he raised his eyes from the paper and looked at his daughter. Vicky searched her father's eyes expectantly, hoping he'd give some clue to the letter's contents. He looked troubled, but his next words were easy and light.

"Look," Ken Loring said, turning to Jeff, "why don't you buy Vicky that *croissant?* We haven't too much time before catching our next plane."

Vicky tapped one toe impatiently. Obviously, her dad wasn't going to reveal anything. Was it because Jeff was here?

"Well," she said to Jeff, "let's not stand here, let's do something about it. I'm dying for one of those marvelous crunchy breakfast rolls and some *café au lait,* and I can't think of a nicer person to have it with." She beamed her best smile at Jeff as she took his arm.

"Git, then," her father said and walked off.

Once the steaming drink of half-coffee, half-milk was set before them, Jeff and Vicky began to talk animatedly. Vicky answered his endless questions about New York and their mutual friends there.

All at once the chatter subsided. Vicky noted the serious look which moved like a cloud into Jeff's eyes. She suspected that his talk would turn to business, and she was right.

"Tell me a little about your father's assignment in Zourab," Jeff inquired. "What's the main story he's after?"

"Uh, uh. Mustn't pry. Didn't you hear Dad say he wasn't giving any interviews at this time? Let's not make like 'Scoop' Hubbell. I have no intention of letting you worm a story out of me," Vicky replied with a slightly scolding tone.

"I'm not trying to. I'm . . . I'm just a little perturbed, that's all."

"Perturbed? Perturbed about what? Zourab is one of those 'little-but-oh-my' countries that the world is suddenly interested in because of its oil deposits and the wonderful contrast between ancient customs and modern times. We're going to cover the whole story, including the archeological expedition at Kalpaz, and that's all," Vicky explained.

"O.K., O.K.," Jeff backed down before Vicky's positive words. "I'm probably imagining burglars under the bed like an old maid. But take care, honey chile, take care."

Vicky stared at Jeff. In spite of the light tone of his

voice, his eyes were grave. Was there something about Zourab that she didn't know? Why had he used the word "perturbed"?

Well, she was going to find out—and soon.

# 2

# Bagara Banquet

"DAD, are you sure we're bound for Zourab and not the moon?" Vicky poked her father and pointed one finger earthward. The ground skimming under the small plane's nose was a wasteland of sand. Desert winds had swirled the brown sand into shadowy dunes. Not a tree or a shrub or life of any kind could be seen. "Doesn't it look exactly like pictures we've seen of the craters of the moon? Ugh!" Vicky shuddered. "Bleak, isn't it?"

"It certainly doesn't look earthly. I agree it wouldn't be hard to think we were passing over another planet," her father replied.

26

"I expected desert, of course, but somehow I thought it would look romantic. You know, white sand gleaming under a huge moon and sheiks in flowing robes on prancing Arabian horses."

"Like the movies, you mean," her father added.

"Well, not really. But *some* kind of life," Vicky said. "But I'm getting a bird's-eye view, I know. When I did my research on Zourab I discovered there are all kinds of nomadic tribes that live on the desert. It can't be quite so bleak at ground level."

"I expect not. But look again. Didn't you learn that Zourab was a land of contrasts?" Her father directed Vicky's gaze toward the plane's window.

The eerie landscape had disappeared. Vicky caught her breath. "It's fairyland—or at least the Land of Oz!" Slender white towers strung with golden globes reached toward them. Peacock-blue domes flashing with gilt seemed to spin by.

"It's like looking down on a pile of gigantic Christmas ornaments," Vicky said excitedly. She could see the tops of palms waving gracefully, and moving dots —many bustling dots—which had to be people.

Vicky crossed over to the window on the other side of the plane. As they came closer to the city, she could see that the buildings spread toward the coastline. A harbor, curved like a scimitar, cut into the land. The deep blue of the water was sprinkled with the bright confetti of colored sails on tiny boats—blue, red, bright yellow.

"Bagara!" she exclaimed. "Is it, Dad? Is it? Are we there?"

"Yep," her father said crisply. "The capital city of Zourab in all its exotic beauty. Your magic carpet has arrived."

Vicky was at the door of the plane almost the moment the small craft touched down, eager to get her first glimpse of this fascinating city. The air terminal building, modern and efficient-looking, was decorated with brightly colored mosaics, blending new architecture with ancient art. Vicky had an impression of whirling color laced with white as she swept a glance over the people in the airport. Many of the women wore white over-garments which swathed them from head to hem. Others wore wide skirts in richly colored brocades. Light scarves in brilliant hues were draped about their heads and shoulders. Some men were dressed in ordinary business suits; others wore long striped garments; almost all wore the white *kaffiyeh* ornamented with jewels and dangling beads.

The air was filled with high voices babbling a sing-song Arabic dialect. Now and then, she heard a greeting in French.

"Welcome to Zourab, to Bagara, to our land, and to our hearts." The words were in a clipped, almost British accent, and Vicky was startled to hear them in this hodgepodge of strange noises.

Vicky switched her purse and flight bag to her left hand and extended her right to the man who stood before her. The man did not take Vicky's hand. Instead, he touched his forehead and his chest lightly and gracefully, and bowed to her.

"I am Monsieur L-Hassa, at your service, Mademoiselle."

Monsieur L-Hassa straightened and extended his hand in a typical American greeting to Ken Loring. "Delighted to meet you in person at last," Ken said. "Both my daughter and I look forward to an interesting visit in Zourab."

With the formalities over, M. L-Hassa hurried them to a waiting car, a gleaming American Cadillac, the very latest model. The car swung through the narrow, teeming streets, past little carts drawn by donkeys and walking women carrying fat bundles on their heads. As they rode, M. L-Hassa outlined the plans for the evening.

"The Shah wishes to honor you and Mademoiselle Victoria with a dinner at the palace tonight. He must leave tomorrow on pressing government business, but he has commanded me to place all the imperial services at your disposal. Once you have settled into your hotel rooms and dressed for dinner, I shall send a car to bring you to the palace."

The big car glided to a stop and M. L-Hassa, with a few short orders and a brief snapping of his fingers, had the Lorings and all their baggage established in the Zourab hotel. And then, almost without warning, he disappeared. Vicky was suddenly reminded of the messenger in Paris. "The vanishing Zourabians," she said to her father. "I wonder if they do it with mirrors."

"It's quite a trick," Ken Loring admitted. "It certainly eliminates the prolonged good-by, doesn't it?"

"Dad, just who is this M. L-Hassa? Obviously he's important," Vicky inquired.

"Aba L-Hassa is the Shah's right hand. Officially, he is the Chief Counsel. In another country he'd probably be called prime minister. He is intensely loyal to the Shah, and the ruler leans heavily on him for advice and guidance."

"Oh, I *am* impressed. Fancy being under the personal care of Mr. Big. I can't wait to let Mr. Jeff Hubbell know how *très* VIP I've become."

"You'll be *très* L-A-T-E if you don't hop to it and start getting dressed for the big show. Wear your best thingamajig, honey."

"Mr. Loring! Aunt Ellen would positively take off like a rocket after you if she could hear you refer to my newest blue chiffon as a 'thingamajig'! And if you could see the bill for it, you'd take off after *me*," Vicky said airily.

"Nevertheless, scamper—get ready." Ken Loring pushed Vicky toward the door. "And I'm sure you'll look lovely, whatever I call it," he added with a smile.

She started in a mock run to her own room, then stopped short.

"Dad, seriously for a moment. What was the message you got at Orly? Wasn't it delivered by a Zourabian? What did it say? My guess is it upset you." Vicky thought that if she asked several questions at once, she might get the answer to at least one of them.

Ken Loring faced his daughter. Vicky watched him carefully as he started to speak solemnly, then changed his mind. "Oh, that. Just some travel directions from M. L-Hassa," he finally replied. "Come on, come on. Get thee going," he ordered hastily.

Vicky got. No sense now in probing further. Dad simply wasn't about to tell her the whole truth. But why? Why? She would have to dig into the matter later.

"Just now, His Imperial Majesty El Mohama Shah-ja requests the honor of my presence at a slight blast he's giving." Vicky giggled at her own incongruous thought. "Aunt Ellen would have a fit if she knew I'd referred to the Shah's dinner as a 'blast.'"

She began to change hurriedly.

The entrance to the palace was breathtaking. The white marble shape, filigreed as intricately as fine lace, was reflected in a huge pool dotted with peacock-blue lights set like gems about it.

Inside, Vicky and her father walked down a wide corridor of pointed arches, each one bordered in an elaborate design. The point of each arch bore a gilt crest which glinted in the light from the crystal chandeliers. Through the last arch, Vicky noted the elegant beauty of a curving white staircase.

Monsieur L-Hassa joined them silently. With great pomp, the Lorings were announced to the Shah, and escorted to the great throne where he sat. He was dressed in brilliant blue from the top of his bejeweled turban to the tips of his embroidered slippers. Vicky noted the warmth in his eyes in spite of his very majestic appearance.

M. L-Hassa gently pulled Vicky aside and motioned her out of the Shah's presence. Ken Loring stayed with the Shah.

"Women are allowed only briefly in the throne

room," he explained. "Your father will stay and speak with His Imperial Majesty. But for you, I have, I think, a pleasant surprise." M. L-Hassa smiled broadly at the girl. "Come this way."

He opened a scarlet and gilt door to a tiny room, luxuriously furnished in pale satins and velvets. Seated on a low bench was a tiny girl. Vicky could only think of the collection of dolls from around the world she had had as a child. The exquisite girl seemed to have been brought to life from the collection. She wore a gold lamé dress with a many-petticoated skirt. Her soft brown hair was pulled back under a gossamer head shawl with gold embroidery. Her huge amber-colored eyes were ringed with black, black lashes.

The golden doll rose gracefully. "Hello," she said in a tinkling voice, just barely touched with an accent. "You must be Victoria. Me, I am Yasmin. Forgive me," she said aside to her father, who looked shocked by her informal introduction. "I should have waited for you to introduce me. Victoria—" she began.

"Vicky," Vicky interrupted. "Just call me Vicky." She beamed at the tiny girl, liking her immediately. "But I feel like a giant clod standing beside her," she thought. "She's so marvelously dainty."

M. L-Hassa stepped forward. "Miss Loring, my daughter Yasmin, who cannot seem to wait for a polite introduction." He tried to look reprovingly at Yasmin but succeeded only in showing his fondness for his doll-like daughter.

"Father, may Vicky and I—how do you say it," Yasmin poised a tiny finger on her cheek, "have a girltalk?" M. L-Hassa raised his eyes to the ceiling as if defeated by Yasmin's ultra-modern talk, but smiled at both girls and left the room.

"How's my American, Vicky? When I went to school in Switzerland, a girl from your country was my roommate. She used to give me lessons. O.K., huh?"

"Perfect. On the nose," Vicky assured her. "But I must admit your American threw me off a bit. I had been thinking you looked like Scheherazade, and I fully expected you to spin me a magical tale or play a lute or something."

"Those things I can do, too," Yasmin said. "I truly am very Zourabian, and I am proud of it. But I like everything I hear about your country and want to visit it some day. Having you here will be the next best thing. We'll have a . . . a . . . dance?" Yasmin finished questioningly.

"A 'ball,' " Vicky corrected.

The two girls laughed together and began to chat. Yasmin's questions about America were followed swiftly by Vicky's questions about Zourab.

A knock on the door interrupted their conversation. A servant in magnificent livery entered and in his musical native language spoke to Yasmin.

"We're to join the others," she translated. "Let us go now, please." She pattered out of the room, her gauzy headdress streaming behind her.

The banquet room held a long table, only eighteen inches from the floor. On each side were placed huge soft cushions, tasseled and embroidered. There were many other guests, all of whom wanted to meet the renowned American and his daughter.

At last, however, the introductions were over and Yasmin gracefully sat down, her legs crossed in front of her. Vicky squatted beside her, having difficulty arranging a comfortable position because of her heeled shoes.

A serving maid came noiselessly to Vicky's side and held out a gold basin. Following Yasmin's example, Vicky stretched her hands over the basin. Perfumed water, poured out of a slender vase, splashed over Vicky's hands. The serving maid wiped Vicky's hands with a snowy-white linen towel.

"How *very* luxurious," she whispered to Yasmin.

"An old custom," Yasmin whispered back.

More serving maids appeared, bearing great platters of food. And what food! Whole roasted lambs were placed at intervals along the long table. There was eggplant stuffed with partridge, rice with saffron and raisins, rice dotted with green pistachio nuts.

Yasmin explained each dish and the Zourabian method of eating. The thin bread was the only utensil. By taking a piece of the bread and pinching each delectable morsel, the food could be brought to the mouth and popped in, bread and all.

Vicky ate hungrily but watched with amazement the quantity the tiny Yasmin was able to consume. Finally the dessert, luscious pink melon, ended the great feast. The servants reappeared with more perfumed water for their guests.

Then the booming of a huge gong announced the entertainment. Tall, muscular men, stripped to the waist, wearing voluminous trousers rich with embroidery, marched out. They carried gleaming mahogany clubs, mammoth and heavy. To the strains of a high monotonous chant, they swung the clubs in rhythm, flung them through the air at one another, and did amazing tricks with them.

Vicky was enchanted. She glanced at her father down the table. He gestured with his hands. Vicky got the message. Such a performance would be an interesting bit for their documentary. She'd make a note of it later.

Eventually, the dinner and its entertainment came to an end. M. L-Hassa and Ken Loring joined the girls and tried to hustle them toward the waiting automobiles.

Yasmin couldn't seem to end the evening. "Vicky," she called, as her father's car moved away, "don't do anything tomorrow until you hear from me. We'll go shopping—Zourabian style."

# 3

# The Bazaar

VICKY jumped in surprise as she opened the door. The first light knock this morning hadn't signaled anything more than the arrival of her breakfast. And now here was a miniature ghost! The diminutive figure was clothed from head to toe in a white garment edged with a fine design in gold. All Vicky could see were amber eyes ringed with sooty black.

"Yasmin!" Vicky cried as she recognized her new friend. "Whatever are you wearing?"

Yasmin released the white garment from her face. "It's a *chador*. See? We wear it over our other clothes." Yasmin flung the garment aside as she pirouetted into the room. Underneath the loose garment she wore a slim, melon-colored sheath, simple and smart as any in an American fashion magazine. "The *chador* protects our clothes—and us—from the sun, the dust . . . the works," she explained. "Here, I've brought one for you."

"I hope it's not one of *yours*," Vicky said with a laugh. "It will look like a bolero on me."

"Yasmin thinks of everything. I borrowed one of my mother's. She's a giant like you."

"Show me how to wear it," Vicky requested.

"Just put it on, like so."

Vicky put the sheetlike gown around her head and about her body.

"Good," Yasmin approved. "Now, to be a real Zourabian woman, hold it like this," and she demonstrated the proper way to clutch the flowing gown.

"But when I opened the door all I could see were your eyes," Vicky said. "Show me that trick, too."

"Oh, I was being very, very Zourabian then. The veil we women used to be forced to wear has been outlawed by the Shah for many years now. But we still like to hide our faces at times and we do so by clenching a bit of the *chador* in our teeth. Like so." Yasmin popped some of the fabric into her mouth and held it across her face with her teeth. "Try it."

Vicky ran to the mirror in the room and practiced. "Howthith?" Vicky mumbled. She turned around for Yasmin's approval.

Yasmin giggled. "Now you know why a Zourabian man who's angry at his woman says, 'Hide thy face.' See? With a mouthful of *chador*, she can't talk."

Vicky exploded with laughter. "Men! They're the same all over the world. Still trying to keep women quiet. Why don't they give up!"

"Oh, I like that. When Hakim tells me to hide my face, I'll say, 'Why don't you give up!'"

"And who's Hakim?" Vicky asked.

"My fiancé," the girl answered. "Or should I say 'my boy friend'?" she asked seriously.

"No, you're right the first time. If you really are going to marry him, we'd say fiancé in America, too." Vicky decided to cut short the language and the *chador* lessons. "Let's get going. I'm anxious to see Bagara."

The two girls, both in their white *chadors*, with only their typically Western high heels showing, headed toward the street and the Bagara bazaar.

Yasmin and Vicky threaded their way through the clamor and color of the street leading to the bazaar.

"Here we are," Yasmin pointed out.

Vicky gazed down the long, thin, brick structure roofed with pointed arches. Here and there, openings at the top of the arch let in the daylight. The thin sprays of light fell like a shower on the heads of the crowds passing under them.

Once Vicky's eyes were used to the gloom after the bright sunlight, she could see that unshaded electric light bulbs illuminated some of the stalls. A constant din of sing-song voices and shouts rose from all corners of the bazaar, making a rumble against the piercing notes of native flutes.

The individual stalls of the bazaar were rich with spicy smells. Here was a spice merchant, seated cross-legged on a mound of rugs, constantly urging customers to stop and buy. His chant never ended, even when he stopped to scoop spice into a cone of paper for a purchaser.

The girls wandered down the long alley, past the barrels of rice, the mounds of pistachio nuts, the heaps of green striped melons. Smiling vendors urged them to buy, holding out their products and chattering in Zourabian about the supreme quality of their wares.

Vicky bought a cone of pistachio nuts and munched them as she wandered about, her observant eyes taking in the scene about her. The stalls had now changed. Here were merchants with clothing, jewelry, and baubles. Vicky stood enchanted before the rug weaver's stall. The brilliance of design and color took away her breath—blues, golds, reds blended wildly but pleasingly. What marvelous pictures could be taken here! She must remember everything to report to her father.

Swept up in the colors, sounds, and smells, Vicky darted from one stall to another.

"Yasmin," she said excitedly, "I could spend a month here. Shopping Zourabian style is tremendous!"

"I'm glad. So many visitors my father takes here complain about the noise and confusion. I'm glad you're not like that," Yasmin said seriously. "But let's take—what do you call it—a break? Right here."

Vicky followed the girl as she walked under a gaudy canopy held up by two intricately carved wooden poles. Pillows were scattered around low tables that were really brass trays on carved teak stands. Yasmin plopped down and clapped her hands. Vicky sat beside her.

A man in a long tunic approached them. Swiftly, Yasmin gave an order in her native language. Almost immediately, delicately carved cups of hot tea were placed before them.

"The cups look more like vases," Vicky said. "No handles. How do we drink from them?"

"So," replied Yasmin, grasping the thin stem with the thumb and index finger of each hand and raising the cup to her lips with a delicate movement.

Vicky caught on quickly and was able to tilt the warm tea toward her mouth.

"*Very* good," Yasmin applauded. "Hardly anybody gets the hang of it so fast. You are really an excellent pupil."

"Tell me about your fiancé, Hakim," Vicky said, settling down for a relaxing chat.

"Oh, he's . . ."

The sound of a shrill whistle knifed into the hubbub of the bazaar.

"A police whistle!" Vicky gasped. "It *must* be."

"It is," Yasmin said quite calmly.

"Aren't you interested in knowing what it's about?"

"Probably some petty thief. The bazaar is always full of them. No one ever pays any attention," the girl added off-handedly.

Vicky looked about her. Yasmin was right. The crowds in the bazaar continued about their business, wandering from stall to stall making purchases. No one had even looked up.

"In New York, everyone would be headed toward the sound of the whistle. We're great rubber-necks," Vicky said.

"Rubber . . . necks?" Yasmin frowned in puzzlement. "A neck of rubber? This I don't understand."

"See, like this." Vicky stretched her neck out and

swiveled it. "We always have to see what's going on, everywhere."

Yasmin's lilting laugh bubbled out. "Oh, I shall have such great fun teasing Hakim. When he starts inquiring too much into where I've been and what I've been doing all day, I shall call him a rubber-neck."

Vicky did not answer. Her attention had been caught by a surge in the crowd outside the tea pavilion. The people bustling through the alley parted as two policemen, in uniforms of the peacock blue which seemed to be Zourab's official color, passed by. Between them was a white-coated figure. "A woman in a *chador* or a man in a white tunic?" Vicky asked herself. She was not able to see through the crowd. The three passed by and out of the bazaar.

Yasmin, who had paid no attention whatsoever to the scene, bounced up from the pillow energetically. "Come, Vicky, I'll show you my favorite stall. Perhaps you'd like to buy a *zada* or two. I think you'll like them. Me, I can't resist them."

"*Zada?*" Vicky replied. "Don't even tell me what it means. Just by the lovely sound of the name I know I'll want several."

Yasmin threw some coins on the low table, and the two girls plunged into the sea of people in the bazaar.

The *zada* stall was aflame with color. The beautiful

head scarves, or *zadas,* hung in festoons about the walls. The slightest breeze made the soft fabrics sway and shimmer like dancing firelight.

"Oooh," Vicky gasped. "Gorgeous, gorgeous," she exclaimed as the merchant spread scarf after scarf before her in enchanting splashes of color.

Vicky couldn't stop. The gauzy scarves with their beautiful borders were perfect gifts.

"I'll take this for Aunt Ellen. And this one for Julia. And this for Lauralee Bartlett back at CBC. Maybe she can even use it on her program. Oh, and this and this for little ole me! Yasmin, what a find! These are divine!" Quickly, Vicky shrugged out of her *chador* and draped the *zadas* around her neck, exclaiming at the bright colors and patterns.

Yasmin smiled. "I knew you'd . . . you'd . . . flop," she finished triumphantly.

"I think you mean 'flip,'" Vicky corrected. "But in a way you're right. My pocketbook will flop after I pay for these." Vicky swirled the *zadas* about her. "But who cares?"

In high spirits, the girls started out of the stall. "We'd better get back to the hotel. We're supposed to meet Dad for tea this afternoon," Vicky announced. "You'd better lead me out quickly, Yasmin. If I find another marvelous stall like this, I'll never leave."

Yasmin scurried ahead, making a path through the crowd. Vicky followed, carrying her *chador* and the gay bundle of *zadas*. Almost at the end of the arcade which housed the bazaar, the crowds began to thin out. The shaft of light streaking through the gap in the high, vaulted ceiling glinted on something on the ground.

Vicky stopped short and picked up the something. She brushed the dust from it with her hand and examined it more closely. It was a button—a large, unevenly round, thick button, golden in color and heavily embossed with a raised design.

"Look, Yasmin. How interesting. It's a button, I think, but like no button I've ever seen before."

Yasmin examined the golden object. "Mmm, seems to me I've seen one like this before." She paused and cocked her head thoughtfully. "Can't think right now. It's really not a button," she added. "It's just been made into one. Actually, it's a little perfume container —the kind Zourab women used to hold, so, in their hand when they went visiting. Tourists like to buy them for souvenirs and, as you see, they can be made into buttons. This is genuine. An old one, not the cheap imitations made for the tourist trade."

"Well, shouldn't I try to find out who lost it and return it?" Vicky asked.

"However could you?" Yasmin replied airily. "Keep it as a souvenir of the Bagara bazaar."

"Well," Vicky hesitated, then made up her mind. "I shall."

The exit lay before them. They walked briskly toward it, and out into the street leading to the hotel. The crowds were much thinner here.

Attracted by the swish of feet behind her—feet keeping pace with her own stride—Vicky glanced over her shoulder. A dark, sinister-looking man in Zourabian garb was at her heels. His cold, ugly eyes looked menacingly into hers before he ducked out of sight in a nearby doorway. There had been something so threatening about the look in his eyes that Vicky shivered.

"What's the matter with me?" Vicky thought to herself. "Why on earth should I have imagined that awful man was following me?" With a shrug, she dismissed the idea. But the nagging thought persisted . . . *had* he been following her?

# 4

# The Woman
# in the News

ON THE walk back to the hotel, Vicky had begun to make plans for Yasmin to really get to know Ken Loring over a congenial afternoon tea. But on their arrival at the hotel, Vicky and Yasmin had been met by Yasmin's old nursemaid. Treating Yasmin like a naughty child, she had hurried her out to a waiting car without any explanation except that Yasmin was to "return home quickly, quickly."

The abruptness of Yasmin's departure had left Vicky with a let-down feeling. And a worried one. Had something happened at the L-Hassa home? Was anything wrong?

Vicky tried to shake off the thoughts, but they kept getting mixed up with her memory of the man in the street, his sinister, staring eyes and his furtive manner.

"Come now, girl," she scolded herself. "There's probably a perfectly logical explanation for both things. The bazaar was crowded with people and that man was probably in a hurry to get somewhere. Just because you're in Zourab and it's strange and unfamiliar, there's no need to look for burglars under the bed."

The words flashing through her mind had a familiar ring. Of course! Jeff had used the very same expression when he talked so seriously to her yesterday morning at the airport in Paris.

"Take care," he had cautioned.

"Snap out of it," Vicky continued to scold herself. "This kind of thinking will get you nowhere except into a slump."

At a quiet dinner that night with her father, her gloom lifted. Ken Loring listened eagerly to Vicky's description of Bagara and her ideas for photographing the bazaar.

"Tomorrow will be a busy day for both of us," Ken Loring said. "The camera crew checked in today. I'm anxious to get them started."

"I know," Vicky agreed. "Yasmin has promised me

a tour of the Shah's palace. I'll make a schedule of shots and a diagram of the camera angles. Ought to be a full day's shooting there."

"Good. See you both in the tea pavilion here when you've finished."

Yasmin appeared at Vicky's door early the next morning. When Vicky asked her about her hurried departure the afternoon before, the reply was airy.

"Oh, that old nursemaid of mine. Everything is a ... a big deal ... with her. Mother simply wanted me because my favorite uncle had arrived from Paris and was leaving for a tour of his oil fields. It was my only chance to see him for months."

Vicky was relieved that her worrying had been unnecessary, but she said nothing.

The day at the palace was busier than Vicky had expected. Yasmin turned out to be an efficient and seemingly tireless guide and her inside knowledge of the palace was tremendously helpful.

"Let's keep that tea date with Dad," Vicky sighed as she flung herself into the back seat of the car she and Yasmin had been using. "I'm bushed."

Yasmin spoke to the driver, and the girls were whisked toward the hotel.

"You go on in ahead," Vicky suggested to Yasmin.

"See if my father has appeared. I want to pick up a newspaper."

Vicky walked toward a small stand where a wizened little man sat, a pile of thin newspapers before him. Vicky glanced at the top paper. The fancy, curving dashes and dots of the Zourabian script met her eyes.

"Well, I'll never know what all the news that's fit to print in Zourab is," she decided, "but I simply can't get through the day without buying a newspaper. I can look at the pictures, at least."

"How much?" she indicated to the little old man in sign language. The newspaper vendor smiled and held up a small Zourabian coin. Vicky fished into her pocket, found its match, and placed it in the skinny palm held out to her. She strolled away, glancing at the paper as she went.

She stopped short, caught by the news picture on the front page. The picture was fuzzy and poorly reproduced, but it flashed a vivid memory in her mind. Here were the two policemen she had seen yesterday in the bazaar and the figure between them was a woman—a woman wearing an odd coat, almost like a *chador*.

Vicky stepped over to a better-lighted spot and examined the newsprint, focusing on an oddly shaped blob in the picture. Could it be? It was! The object on the woman's coat was a strangely shaped button, a button very much like the gold one she had found in the Bagara bazaar. "I'm almost positive!" she said aloud.

She hurried toward the tea pavilion.

"Yasmin," she called as she came near the girl, seated alone at a tea table. "Look at this!" She pushed the newspaper across the table. "Translate the caption under it for me, will you?"

Yasmin's face registered polite interest, then shock. "Oh, no. It cannot *be!*"

"Look. Look very closely. Isn't that button on the woman's coat like the one I found yesterday?" Vicky urged. "Who is the woman? What does the story say about her?"

"I cannot believe it. The paper says that Pamela Wilson has been arrested. I simply cannot believe it." Yasmin's repeated disbelief clearly indicated her shock at the news.

"Why? Who is she?" Vicky pursued impatiently but politely.

"Well, it doesn't really say 'arrested.' It says she has been taken in for questioning."

"Is that *all?*" Vicky questioned. "There's no story about it?"

Yasmin read hurriedly. "That's all. Our one and only

newspaper isn't as complete as your big New York journals are."

"But you know who the woman is. Tell me about her."

"Well, Pamela Wilson is the wife of the British archeologist Reginald Wilson," Yasmin began.

"Archeologist! Then they're out at Kalpaz with the expedition Dad is going to put into his documentary," Vicky said.

"That's right. Kalpaz was the site of our ancient capital, thousands of years ago. The Shah is very much interested in the 'dig,' or excavation, there. My father entertained Mr. and Mrs. Wilson on the Shah's orders when they first arrived. He put his stamp of approval on all their plans. I can't understand why the police would be interested in Mrs. Wilson." Yasmin shook her head, puzzled. "Everything about the Wilsons' project is in order—or was."

"Is Mrs. Wilson an archeologist, too?" Vicky asked.

"No, I don't think so. She is sort of a recorder, I guess you'd say. She makes a note of each thing that's found, draws maps and diagrams of the dig . . . things like that," Yasmin finished.

"What kind of a person is she?" All of Vicky's reporter's instincts were alive. "There's a story here," she said to herself.

"Oh . . . she's nice. Pretty, in a wishy-washy way," Yasmin said slowly. "I don't really know her, Vicky, but I can't picture her doing anything bad. But perhaps it was a mistake."

"Do you know her well enough to go see her, to go wherever they are holding her?" Vicky demanded.

"I guess so—and my father . . ."

"Could give us official permission to see her," Vicky finished. "Couldn't he?"

Yasmin didn't answer the question. "Here comes *your* father, now," she said instead. "And my Hakim is with him." Her eyes filled with delight. She smiled and clapped her tiny hands.

"Oh, dear," Vicky thought glumly, "the whole thing has popped out of her mind."

Ken Loring, accompanied by a young man, arrived at the table.

"Vicky," he said, "may I present Hakim-Bandor. He's been my official guide for the day and he's been an enormous help. Yasmin, I take it you have met Hakim."

"Met!" she said, startled. "Didn't he tell you he's my . . ." She broke off her words. "Oh, I see now, it is a joke." Her laugh tinkled.

"A pretty feeble one," Ken admitted, "but it's big in Zourab, judging from your laugh. Oh, yes, Hakim has been bending my ear all day about you two and your wedding plans."

Vicky studied Yasmin's fiancé. He was dressed in a light, Western-style suit, very correctly tailored, and wore an elaborate brocade turban on his head. From the way it was wrapped and from the gold insignia Vicky knew he must be the son of an important sheik. She'd read a little about Zourabian "nobility" before her trip to Bagara.

"*Enchanté,*" Hakim said, and continued in perfectly accented French, "I hope Yasmin has not chattered like a monkey at you all day. She is enchanting but noisy."

Vicky answered him in French, surprised to find that her words rolled out fluently. "I find her absolutely enchanting, and as for noise, I fear that I am something of a chatterbox myself."

"*Les femmes, les femmes,*" Hakim said with a mock sigh, his dark brown eyes gleaming.

"What an adorable couple they will make," Vicky thought, observing the slim, not too tall, handsome young man.

The tea in delicate cups had arrived and with it sweet pastry cakes, dripping with honey and stuffed with nutmeats. Vicky realized she was very hungry and wolfed down two. "Ooooh," she commented, "afternoon tea in Zourab better not be a habit. I'll have to diet for a month."

The talk at the table continued to be light, polite, and social. Hakim was well-informed about his country's history, its art, and its customs. Under Vicky's and Ken Loring's questioning he gave color to the knowledge they already had of Zourab and added more information to it. Finally, he rose and extended his arm to Yasmin.

"Come, little bird, my ancient grandfather wishes to see us." She reached up and allowed him to pull her from the cushions.

"Very well, Hakim, but after that I must go directly home. I need the closed eye." She grinned at Vicky, so pleased with herself that Vicky didn't have the heart to correct her. "Besides," Vicky thought, "why not 'closed eye' as well as 'shut-eye'?"

When the couple had gone, Vicky leaned toward her father intently. "Dad, there's a picture in today's local paper and I want to tell you . . ."

"Hold it for the moment, princess. I have a job for you to do, or, at least, try to do. You may have to go to Monsieur L-Hassa on it, and perhaps Yasmin can get you to him conveniently. I want you to see what you can find out about the arrest yesterday of the wife of a British archeologist working at the Kalpaz dig."

Vicky managed to conceal a smile as she dug a pencil and note pad from her handbag.

"Righto, Mr. Boss, fill me in on it," she said brightly. Then she added to herself, "But I'll bet I'm way ahead of you."

# 5

## Button, Button

From each end of the low white building rose fat, onion-shaped domes, brilliantly enameled in peacock blue. Tall shafts piercing each dome were topped by the flag of Zourab, colorful as a *zada*.

"We'll go in the far entrance, near my father's office," Yasmin said.

The entrance hall was cool after the noon heat outside. Huge fans, attached to the low ceiling, swished monotonously.

Vicky walked briskly, sure that the desk at the end of the hall was her proper target. Yasmin pattered along behind her, explaining. "That's Najeeb at the

58

desk, one of my father's secretaries. We have to see him first. He's very jealous of his authority and won't even permit me to see my father until he announces me. He gives me an ache, sometimes."

"Pain," Vicky corrected automatically, intent on her mission.

Serious as she felt, Vicky almost burst into laughter as she looked at the man. Above the gleaming white teeth revealed by an enormous artificial smile was the widest mustache she had ever seen. Black and waxed, it stretched four inches on either side of Najeeb's round face, curling upward past his nose.

The short, fat man leaped from behind his desk, bowing in short, jerky bobs. "Welcome, a thousand welcomes, to the office of Najeeb, secretary important to the great leader, Aba L-Hassa," he intoned in one breath without stopping between words.

"Really, Najeeb, you don't have to be so flowery every time I come in here. Where is my father? We should like to see him." Yasmin was curt, having put away her doll-like charms.

"Your illustrious father," Najeeb mused, his head held to one side, thinking, "is a very busy man this morning. Many calls he must make to other important figures here in our ministry building. Najeeb must see that he is not disturbed except for good cause."

"This *is* good cause," Yasmin said firmly.

The man shot an exasperated glance at Vicky. The mustache ends quivered with indignation.

"Najeeb decides what cause is good, what cause is bad," he said with self-importance.

Yasmin tapped the toe of her tiny shoe with impatience. "Try to reach him; we must see him immediately," she ordered.

The smiling and bowing began once again. "But, of course, for you, Mademoiselle."

The man picked up an ornate telephone near his hand and began to bark orders into it. Again he smiled, apparently pleased with the swiftness with which his orders were obeyed.

"I am sorry," he said after he had repeated the telephoning process two or three times. "I am unable to establish his whereabouts. Aha, but for you I shall try one more place."

With a great sweep of his hand, he brushed some papers aside and started to pick up the phone again. Vicky saw the glint of metal and heard a clatter as an object rolled from under the papers onto the hard top of the desk.

For an instant she saw it. There was no mistaking that shape. It was another button like her bazaar find, like the button on Pamela Wilson's strange coat!

Smooth as a snake's slither, Najeeb's hand reached out and palmed the button like a magician. He continued barking into the phone transmitter.

Vicky blinked. The appearance and disappearance of the button had been so swift she could scarcely believe she'd seen it. How could she ask this ferocious little man about it?

He turned his oily smile on her as he replaced the phone. "I am so sorry, Mesdemoiselles. Monsieur L-Hassa is nowhere about. And, Mademoiselle Yasmin's friend, you were curious about this?" He held out a round gold colored disc. "Is it not an interesting little thing?" He pressed a tiny catch in the disc and a slender blade uncurled. "How, you will ask, does this blade curl within the round circle? Clever, very clever, are our Zourabian metalsmiths."

Vicky examined the blade politely. It *was* a fascinating letter opener, if that was what it was. But it definitely was *not* the object she had seen before. Najeeb was purposely trying to distract her attention from the gold button.

He continued smoothly. "A thousand pardons that I am unable to help you this morning. Monsieur L-Hassa is nowhere to be found."

All three heads turned toward a door at one side which had clicked open. Monsieur L-Hassa stood in it.

"Good day," he called cheerily. "What brings you two to my staid office? Aren't there more fascinating sights in Bagara?"

"You-were-there-all-the-time, Master, and-your-humble-servant-knew-it-not-and-has-misled-the-fine-ladies," Najeeb streamed out the words in apology. No one paid any attention to him. Monsieur L-Hassa was already ushering the girls into the inner office.

"Monsieur L-Hassa," Vicky began the moment she was seated, "Father and I are interested in learning more about the reasons Pamela Wilson was taken into custody for questioning. He asked me to see you first, and Yasmin was good enough to bring me here. Can you set us right on it?"

"Immediately. It is nothing, really nothing. A misunderstanding only. I am now in the process of explaining this to the British Consul and she shall be released," Yasmin's father explained.

"Why was she arrested in the first place then?" Vicky persisted.

"As I have said, a misunderstanding. But certain procedures must be followed in our country. There are certain things so different here I should find it too time-consuming to explain," Monsieur L-Hassa shrugged at the whole affair. His tone suddenly changed. "I have it! Why don't you girls go to see Mrs. Wilson, cheer her with the encouraging news, visit with her, see if she desires anything."

"Oh, yes," Yasmin chirped enthusiastically. "Let's do that."

Vicky wasn't at all satisfied with Monsieur L-Hassa's explanation. She began to think of further questions which might dig out more information. Quickly, she decided against using them. Yasmin's father could always pull his official rank on her and then she'd be nowhere. But at least she could see Pamela Wilson and find out what she could from her. "The *mysterious* Middle East," she thought, "has nothing on the *muddled* Middle East."

"Well?" Yasmin said, breaking into her thoughts.

"Oh, yes. Of course. I'd like to meet Pamela Wilson. Let's do go," Vicky answered.

The jailer was sullen and sleepy and waved the girls off with a listless don't-bother-me gesture. Yasmin held up the official card her father had given her. The man sprang to attention, saluted with the Zourabian hand-on-forehead-and-chest bow, and tripped over his own feet as he opened the gates to let them in.

The girls walked through the dark stone corridors behind him. He pointed out a clean, cool room that was neatly but sparsely furnished—and barred.

"Here," he said in Zourabian. From the flowing sleeve of his tunic he took a huge ring of keys. He fumbled with them and finally selected one. He opened the barred door and hurled it back. It clanked against the strong bars.

The woman lying on the cot raised her head as the girls entered.

Vicky started to step toward her but was stopped by the sound of the cell door being clicked into position. behind them. The key grated in the lock, and the keeper moved silently away. They were all locked in together.

Vicky saw the figure on the cot rise. The woman stood up and straightened her dress. Vicky was conscious of a white hand brushing back pale blond, straight hair from a milky forehead.

"Why is she so white?" Vicky thought. "She's been out at the dig long enough to have a tan as brown as teakwood."

The woman's pale eyes looked at the girls questioningly. Suddenly, a charming smile lighted her face as she recognized Yasmin.

"You, aren't you Yasmin L-Hassa?" she asked in a soft, warm voice.

"Oh, you remember me," Yasmin said, friendly as a patted puppy. "This is my friend from America, Victoria Loring. My father has sent us to talk with you and cheer you."

"Loring? Loring?" Pamela Wilson asked. She answered her own question. "Of course, daughter of the famous Kenneth Loring. My husband has corresponded with your father about the dig at Kalpaz. I am delighted to meet you."

"Is this a jail or a London tea shoppe?" Vicky thought. The woman did not seem at all distraught. Jail in Zourab might have been her natural habitat.

"Yes," Vicky finally said. "Yasmin's father has asked us to come and tell you that your arrest was a misunderstanding and that he is arranging for your release. I'm sure you'll be glad to know that."

"Naturally," Pamela said crisply. But there was no delight, almost no concern, in her voice.

Vicky examined the woman, trying to figure out her casual attitude.

While Yasmin and Pamela Wilson exchanged pleasant little conversational tidbits, Vicky looked around the cell. Only one small window let in the daylight. The window, like most of those in Zourab, was arched and decorated. But this one was heavily barred.

Underneath the window were several hooks. On one of them hung a limp, white garment. The coat Vicky had seen in the newspaper picture?

Vicky picked it off the hook and broke into the chit-chat being carried on by Yasmin and Mrs. Wilson.

"What an interesting coat!" she said. "It's almost like a *chador*, but not quite."

"But you're so right, my dear," said Pamela. "It was a *chador* but I never *could* get the hang of how to hold the thing about me. So I redesigned it into a coat and had buttons put on it. Most interesting buttons—I must say, I do like buttons, and pockets, in a coat."

"But there aren't any buttons on it now," Vicky said, leading Pamela on.

Pamela took the *chador*-coat from Vicky.

"Aren't there?" she asked anxiously. "Oh, dear," she continued, "and they were *such* interesting buttons. Yul Skersh—he's my husband's colleague on the dig—will be so disappointed. He bought them for me originally, you know," she continued to Vicky.

"Yul Skersh?" Vicky inquired.

"Oh, yes. He's an observer with our group. A most charming man. When I told him I must—I simply must—have buttons on my *chador*, he very gallantly presented me with four of the most intriguing buttons I had ever seen. It seems he found them in one of the bazaar stalls."

"Oh," commented Vicky, "and they've been on your coat ever since?"

"Yes—that is, they *were*. I mean, I didn't notice they were missing until you mentioned it." A frown appeared on Pamela's white forehead. "You know, I have no idea how I could have lost all four of them. And I *must* say I am depressed. They were such charming baubles."

Vicky was just about to tell Pamela of her find in the bazaar, when her alert eyes caught a movement—the merest whisk of a shadow—against the arched window. Her head jerked toward the dim light just in time to see a face peering in at the three of them. Piercing eyes stared briefly into hers, and were gone. It was the man she had seen in the street yesterday! The one who had made her shiver! Had he followed her here? Why? She replaced the coat on the hook and turned to the other two women in the cell.

Vicky's mind was in a turmoil. Should she alert them to this spying danger? Was the face at the window interested in Vicky Loring? Mrs. Wilson? Yasmin? Or all three?

The questions were jolted from Vicky's whirling brain by Mrs. Wilson.

In a quick and anxious movement, Pamela Wilson was at Vicky's side. She clutched Vicky's two arms with her pale, delicate hands.

"You *must* do something for me," she pleaded. The

light, tea-time voice was gone. She seemed deeply agitated.

Vicky tensed, and Yasmin, who had been idly adjusting the *zada* she wore, sat stiff and upright on the cot where she had been lazily stretched. The woman's alarmed voice, the sudden change in her manner, was ominous.

"You *must* get word to Reginald at the dig that I am well and that everything was a misunderstanding and that all will be straightened out soon," Pamela said tensely. "You'll do it for me, won't you?"

Vicky gazed into the woman's pale eyes. Sparks of fear now shot from them.

"Did she see the face, too?" Vicky asked inwardly.

Thoughtfully, she looked at Pamela Wilson, trying to search her face for a clue to this changed behavior.

"We'll try," Vicky finally managed to say.

# 6

## To the Dig

"REALLY, Dad, it's a perfect chance for me to give the dig a once-over. When I get back, we'll know just how much footage we have to give to Kalpaz," Vicky insisted.

Vicky was rushing about the room collecting things. An ornate saddlebag was stretched out on the bed. She stuffed an extra sweater into it. She thrust her hands into the pockets of the riding pants she wore, looking about to see what else she should pack.

Ken Loring was seated on the edge of his chair, elbows on his knees, his chin propped on his folded hands.

"I grant you that, Victoria, but is the trip entirely necessary? It seems to me Reginald Wilson will be informed through normal channels that his wife's arrest is a mistake and that she'll be released soon. Why do *you* have to race off? You've work to do here in Bagara, you know."

"Oh, oh. You're angry," Vicky said, slowing down her packing speed. "That 'Victoria' was the tip-off." She mimicked her father's voice on the "Victoria."

"I'm not angry," Ken replied with emphasis. "I just thought we'd be seeing Kalpaz for the first time together. Might be interesting to see the atomic-age child's reaction to stone-age history." He smiled thinly. "Besides, you still haven't told me about your meeting with Reginald's wife. What's she like?"

"Well," Vicky said slowly, "at first I thought she was terribly chin-up and carry-on-in-spite-of-it-all. But by the time we left her she seemed . . ." Vicky paused. "She seemed almost terrified."

"Nonsense, my girl, what's she got to be terrified about? Though I'll admit a jail anywhere isn't the pleasantest place to be," Ken Loring said.

"I don't know, actually," Vicky replied thoughtfully. Her mind turned over all the events of the past few days. Should she tell her father about the face in the window—and the staring eyes in the bazaar? She decided not to. He'd cancel this trip to Kalpaz in a flash. "Maybe I'll find out at the dig," she finished.

"Did you talk to her about the dig at all?" Ken asked.

"No, not really. She mentioned something about an observer being there—from another country, I think, not from England. A Yul Skersh—I think that's how she pronounced his name. Doesn't sound English."

Ken Loring's face lifted from its comfortable, propped-on-hand position.

"Skersh," he said, "Yul Skersh. Unusual name." Abruptly he rose to his feet and strode about the room. "An observer at the Kalpaz site," he mumbled to himself. With a hint of irritation in his voice, he said to Vicky, "When are Yasmin and Hakim due to pick you up? Best get going—and get back soon," he added in a softer, calmer voice.

A few minutes later, Ken Loring left an affectionate kiss on his daughter's nose and departed. Vicky looked after her father searchingly. "He's been secretive about that letter he received at the airport—and now this peculiar reaction about letting me go to the dig," she thought. "What's *UP?*"

Vicky stood in the middle of the room, lost in thought, her hands jammed into the pockets of her riding pants. Suddenly, among the few coins in her right-hand pocket, she felt the irregular shape of the golden button. She pulled it out slowly and looked at it. Where did the little, intricately worked object fit into the picture?

With vague intentions of finishing her packing job, but with question marks still floating through her mind, she went into the bathroom. Her face, on which the Zourabian sun had already sprinkled a dozen new freckles, stared back at her from the mirror.

"If Jeff Hubbell could see this new crop, he'd laugh himself silly," she thought, and made a face, more at Jeff than at herself.

She placed the button on the small shelf over the sink and picked up her jar of cold cream. As she dabbed her nose and cheeks, the figure of the strange man glided through her mind. All at once her vigorous creaming stopped. Her brown eyes widened as the truth struck her.

"*He wants that button!* That *must* be it!" she said aloud.

Without setting down the cold cream jar, Vicky picked up the golden button. It seemed full of mystery —and danger. Now she was sure the man had seen her pick it up in the market place. Hadn't he spied on her twice? Vicky fought down her panic and tried to think. Suddenly, she was determined. If someone wanted that button, she wanted it, too. Well, she couldn't keep it in her pocket. Whom could she trust to keep it for her? Dad? "No," she decided, "no time now to explain everything to him."

Vicky glanced away from the mirror. Through a nearby window she could see a section of the square in front of the building. As she looked, a jeep made its way from a side street and pushed through the crowded space toward the hotel. At the wheel was Hakim and beside him was Yasmin's tiny figure.

"Here they are! And my bag's not even packed!"

Vicky finished creaming her face and swished off the excess cream with a tissue. Despite her haste, there was a curious smile of secret satisfaction on Vicky's face as she slung her saddlebag over her shoulder and closed the door of her room behind her.

Vicky swung the saddlebag into the back of the jeep and followed it in.

"Yasmin, I must say this is the jazziest saddlebag I've ever seen. Thanks for sending it around," Vicky said gaily.

"It was Hakim's idea. He knew you'd need it. We're going by jeep only as far as Mazzun, that's the nearest oasis to Kalpaz. From there on, it will have to be by horseback," Yasmin declared, "and how could you handle a suitcase on horseback?" She shrugged her shoulders to show how impossible the situation would be.

"Thank you, Hakim. It's truly beautiful. What is it made of?" Vicky inquired as Hakim maneuvered the jeep through the narrow streets.

"The finest of goatskin. It was ornamented by the women of my father's tribe. We are proud to offer it to you. It is yours," the young man said solemnly.

"Oh, I couldn't dream of . . . I didn't mean," Vicky said, flustered. She had forgotten the Zourab custom. If one admired a possession of a Zourabian, the article was immediately presented as a gift. "*Merci mille fois,*" she finally said, hoping that the French reply would make up for her awkwardness.

But Yasmin's chatter covered up for her nicely. "You could use it for a great, huge pocketbook. My American friend at school used to carry one large as so!" She extended her arms as wide as she could.

"You're right," Vicky laughed. "It will be a sensation on Fifth Avenue."

The jeep sped along a narrow but smoothly paved road as the two girls talked animatedly. Hakim drove skillfully. Vicky refused to let Yasmin's steady flow of words prevent her from observing the countryside.

The vegetation became sparser and sparser as they drove along until nothing but sand flowed by the jeep on either side. Atop the dunes, silhouetted against the sky, Vicky could see the outline of camel trains. Far off toward the horizon to her left, she saw a jumble of what looked like small black triangles—hundreds of them. "Oil wells," she surmised.

Jagged mounds of rock now filled the landscape. Again, low brush and stunted palm trees began to dot the sand. Soon, lusher palms appeared and, in the distance, she could see low, white buildings which announced their arrival at Mazzun.

Mazzun was even more crowded than Bagara. The oasis town at the edge of the desert was a crossroads for the old and the new. Camel-train leaders in desert costume mingled with oil workers in thoroughly modern work clothes and protective plastic helmets.

In the market-place café where the three travelers ate a long, late, lunch, Vicky was enchanted by the various Arabic dialects which wove their sing-song thread throughout the café murmur.

"The horses await, master," said a turbaned servant as the group finished their tea.

Hakim rose. "It is time to leave for the desert. The sun is beginning to sink. We shall ride in the cool of the evening."

"Put your *chador* on over your riding clothes," Yasmin suggested. "And you'll probably want to use the trick I taught you. You know, holding it around your face with your teeth. It will keep the blowing sand from your face."

The party rode out in the desert until full night had fallen and the deep blue sky was studded with gleaming stars.

"We sleep," Hakim finally announced.

Vicky pulled the rugs from her horse's back and spread them out, following Yasmin's and Hakim's example. She crept between the rugs, pulled the light *chador* completely over her head, and settled down to sleep. Just before she drifted off, she could almost hear Jeff Hubbell's voice saying, " 'Night. Take care.' "

The bustle of early morning activity came to their ears long before they rode into the headquarters camp at the Kalpaz dig. Vicky, Hakim, and Yasmin had risen in the first light of the day and had ridden hard to beat the sun into Reginald Wilson's camp.

Vicky alighted from her tired horse and turned it over to a servant who popped from nowhere to take it.

Over near a large green tent she could see a man briskly sloshing water from a basin onto his face. The man reached for a towel and rubbed his face. Vicky approached him.

"Reginald Wilson?" she asked, pushing the folds of the *chador* back from her face.

Her guess had to be right. The man's sun-bleached hair and his tall, lanky frame set him apart from the smaller, darker Zourabian workers in the camp.

The man peered out at Vicky from the folds of the towel.

"Righto," came the crisp answer. Then, "I *say!* Who are you? And where on earth did you come from?"

"My name is Vicky Loring and I've just ridden in from Bagara with Yasmin L-Hassa and her fiancé Hakim-Bandor," Vicky replied.

"Whatever for?" Reginald Wilson queried. He scratched his long chin. "Oh, of course," he continued, "your father and I have corresponded about photographing the dig. Where is he? I'm jolly well anxious to meet him."

"He's not here," said Vicky, coming to the point. "I'm—we're here—primarily to bring you a message from your wife."

"From Pam? Then she isn't with you? I'm expecting her back from Bagara today," Reginald Wilson said. "Is anything the matter?"

"Not really," Vicky said, forcing a reassuring smile to her lips. "But, but she's in jail . . ."

"In jail!" The two words exploded from the man. He threw down the towel he had been holding with an angry gesture.

"Oh, but not for long. It was all a misunderstanding, you see. And M. L-Hassa assured me that everything would be cleared up and she would be released just as soon as the red tape could be cut," Vicky sped the words out as fast as she could to quiet his fears.

"Good morning. What have we here?" a deep, guttural voice interrupted.

Vicky wheeled around. A thickly set man, his muscles bulging under the thin cotton shirt he wore, joined Vicky and Mr. Wilson. The new man was dressed in twill riding pants and high riding boots. His closely cropped black hair was stiff and bristly like the small dark mustache over his upper lip. He stood very stiff, his two huge fists held imperiously on his hips.

"Skersh," Reginald barked. "What's this about Pam? Why haven't I been informed?"

"Informed of what?" He spat the last word out and shot a steely glance at Vicky, almost ignoring Wilson's question.

"Informed of his wife's arrest," Vicky replied calmly. Inside, she seethed at Yul Skersh's rude manner.

"Yes," Wilson broke in. "Miss Loring here tells me that Pam has been taken into custody by the authorities in Bagara. Surely you heard something about it over the shortwave. You signaled Bagara yesterday. I heard you. Surely the news would be all over Bagara.

Probably in the press, too. What did Najeeb have to say?"

Najeeb! Yasmin's father's oily secretary. Was he in touch with the camp? Vicky followed Skersh's next words closely.

"Nothing," said Skersh, "except that he would see we got the supplies requested. Reception was very bad on the shortwave. Hardly had I given the supply order when communication went out. The radio is not working."

Reginald Wilson backed down under Skersh's firm stare. "Oh," he decided, "perhaps that is why Pam sent the message here by Miss Loring."

"What is Pamela's trouble?" Skersh asked.

"She's been taken in by the authorities for questioning," Vicky explained, examining Skersh's expression closely. "However, it all seems to be a mistake and M. L-Hassa is straightening things out with the British consulate."

"Well, why do we trouble ourselves?" Skersh said off-handedly. He turned away abruptly and went toward a group of workers who were busy preparing the morning tea.

"Tell me, Mr. Wilson," Vicky said chattily after Skersh had moved a short distance away. "Was your wife in the habit of going to Bagara often?"

"Indeed yes. She went regularly once a week. Just to get away from the dig, you know, and to shop. Went every Tuesday, came back on Wednesday. Picked up light supplies for us. That sort of thing."

"She went the same day? Every week? Did she see any one in particular?" Vicky questioned.

"Not really. Except Najeeb, of course," the man answered.

Vicky noticed that Yul Skersh, a large cup in his hand, a long, thin, oval cigarette dangling from his thick fingers, was strolling about the campsite, circling nearer and nearer to them. His head was strained toward them. "Listening?" Vicky wondered to herself.

"Why did she see Najeeb every week?" Vicky said, lowering her voice.

"Eh?" said Reginald, straining to get the question.

An electronic crackle from one of the tents interrupted them.

Startled, Vicky turned toward the sound. Her eye caught Skersh's hurried movement. He hurled down his tea cup and ran toward the shortwave radio. The "broken" radio, Vicky knew by the sound, was very much alive.

Reginald Wilson didn't answer Vicky's question. A delighted smile lighted his long, hound-dog face. "Good show!" he exclaimed. "Yul must have fixed the shortwave. He's most clever with that sort of thing, you know. It's one reason I like having him on here." And Wilson followed in Skersh's footsteps.

Vicky's hands dropped to her sides. She heaved a sigh.

"Am *I* the odd ball in this group?" she asked herself. "Am *I* the only one who smells the fish?"

Shaking her head in bewilderment, she walked over to the low table where Yasmin and Hakim sat at breakfast.

# 7

# A Matter of Exposure

VICKY sat down on the pile of rugs next to Yasmin with a thump.

"May I have some tea, please, Yasmin? Perhaps it will clear my head."

"You have the head pain?" Yasmin asked solicitously.

"Ache," Vicky said. "No, not really. Just too many unanswered questions knocking together in my noggin, I guess."

"Noggin?" Hakim and Yasmin said in the same breath.

"My head, I mean," Vicky explained.

"Mr. Wilson was glad to hear his wife would soon be released?" Hakim inquired.

"Yes, although he was shocked at first by the news that she'd been arrested."

"He did not know about it before you told him?" Hakim asked, surprised.

"It seems not," Vicky said.

The explanation she started to give was interrupted by Yul Skersh. He strode up to them and bowed smoothly from his waist. "Daughter of Zourab's illustrious Chief Counsel and her fiancé, I understand. Our camp is honored," he said graciously. "I have just learned of your presence here. Otherwise I should have greeted you sooner."

Skersh turned to Vicky. "And you are the daughter of a world-famous American, I have also learned. Forgive my not formally welcoming you before. Morning in the camp is a busy time. I am afraid I forgot my courtesies." He smiled apologetically.

Vicky nodded her head rather stiffly, acknowledging his apology.

"I shall try to make it up to you all," he continued suavely. "Mr. Wilson suggests—and I thoroughly agree —that a trip to the remote section of the dig would be most interesting to you all. I shall be most honored to be your guide."

"Oh, I would love to see it all." Yasmin clapped her hands together. "Please, please Hakim. We don't have to get back to Bagara right away, do we?" she begged.

"Will Mr. Wilson accompany us?" asked Vicky.

"No, he thinks not," Skersh replied. "He will stay in camp today going over the notes, awaiting his wife's arrival. I assure you that I, too, am a trained archeologist and will be able to answer any of your questions."

Hakim-Bandor made the decision. "Very well," he said. "I think it would be a worthwhile trip to take. It would be especially helpful to you and your father, Vicky, would it not?"

"Yes. Yes, it certainly would," Vicky agreed.

The party of four mounted horses and set out across the desert, Yul Skersh in the lead. Vicky spurred her horse and caught up with him. Yasmin and Hakim rode side by side in the rear.

"What is the main purpose of the dig?" Vicky asked.

"Well," Skersh replied, "while we are digging for the remains of an ancient Zourab city, we hope to find traces of an even earlier civilization here. Mr. Wilson has already found flaked flint points, scrapers, and a sicklelike blade. The sickle-blade suggests agriculture as far back as 11,000 years ago."

"Check," Vicky thought. She had asked the question purposely. In one letter to her father, Reginald Wilson had told of these discoveries—and suggested his findings were something he had not told everyone. But Skersh knew about them.

"The farthest point of the dig will be the most interesting," Skersh continued. "It is remote, but well worth the trip. I have been concentrating my efforts in this section. We'll rest, of course, while the sun is high in the sky."

During the midday stopover, Vicky had to admit to herself that Skersh was an interesting character. He told them in a lively, colorful way of travels he had made and strange countries he had visited. He knew the desert, too. The sun shelter he erected was effective. He had brought along water and fruit to refresh them.

But Vicky refused to be lulled into a feeling of complete security. The cold looks he tossed her way every now and then when he thought she wasn't looking were in direct contrast to his solicitous actions. Toward the middle of the afternoon, the party started off again.

"Isn't that the dig up ahead?" Vicky asked after a time.

"You've sharp eyes," Skersh complimented her. "Many people are confused by the shifting light in the desert and cannot make out objects at a distance. Sometimes they see things that are not there."

In a few minutes, they reached a collection of small tents standing in a half circle. Beyond, Vicky could see the top of a large hole in the sand covered with a canvas tarpaulin. No one was in sight and the place had an empty, abandoned look.

As if he had anticipated Vicky's question, Skersh remarked, "A most interesting new excavation at the main dig was opened yesterday. We have ordered all our available workmen from this site back there to explore it."

The four dismounted and began to follow Skersh as he showed them the excavations and explained the methods of digging and the handling of the artifacts as they were unearthed. After a few minutes, Vicky noticed that Skersh had been skillfully moving them away from the tents. Without attracting attention, she detached herself from the group and sauntered toward the nearest of the tents. She casually picked up the flap and walked in.

When her eyes had become adjusted to the faint light filtering through the canvas of the tent, Vicky looked around her. The tent seemed crowded, though it contained only a narrow cot, a small writing table, a folding chair, and a foot locker. Then she noticed that a heavy blanket had been fastened across the rear of the tent.

Swiftly, she stepped to the blanket and pulled it aside. Beyond was a tiny space. To one side, several large spools of wire were stacked on the floor. Against the opposite wall stood some small, heavily constructed crates. But it was the sight of the object in the center of the room that brought a puzzled frown to Vicky's face.

The instrument sat on an overturned crate. Along the front of its light gray case a row of silver knobs and a small dial glittered. Behind a square glass window in the top, Vicky saw a band of ruled graph paper on which a stylus had traced a thin, wavering line. Wires ran from the back of the instrument to a row of storage batteries on the floor.

The sound of rapid footsteps on the sand outside brought Vicky to attention. She stepped toward the front of the tent, letting the blanket fall closed behind her. The front flap of the tent was flung up and Yul Skersh stood glaring in at her.

"Oh! You are curious about my quarters," he said, throwing back the other tent flap and allowing the desert sunlight to pour in. "We live a Spartan life out here. Very few comforts, as you have seen." There was a curious tenseness in his voice as he finished, and Vicky saw his eyes flick for a moment to the blanket at the rear of the tent.

Before Vicky could answer, a cry from outside startled them both.

"Monsieur Skersh!" It was Yasmin's voice. "See what I have found!"

For a second, Skersh remained staring at Vicky, his eyes glittering strangely. Then, suddenly, his whole manner became suavely calm once more.

"Shall we go and see what Mademoiselle L-Hassa has found, Miss Loring?" he said with elaborate politeness. With a bow he permitted Vicky to precede him from the tent.

A moment later, with the others, she was bending over Yasmin's "find." It was a curved metal S with a metal line through it. When Skersh's laughter boomed out, Vicky added hers to it.

"You've found a money clip!" Vicky said, still chuckling. "It's not an ancient treasure. See, it's shaped like an American dollar sign. Many men in the United States use them."

"Yes," said Yul Skersh, "and I am grateful to you for finding it. It is not worth much, but it was given to me by a . . . a friend of mine. I must have dropped it from my pocket."

"You've been to America, then," said Vicky.

"No, it was merely given to me by one who had been there," Skersh said, pocketing the gadget.

"Oh," said Yasmin. I thought it might be an ancient tribe's artifact. But I'm glad I found it for you," she added in a sunny voice.

Yul Skersh continued his lecture on the dig. Vicky listened with only one ear. Her mind was doing research on the instrument she had seen in the small tent.

Her memory clicked. "It's a seismograph!" She had almost said it aloud. "The kind they use for oil exploration," she remembered, her mind now giving her details of a story she had once researched for her father. The four of them continued their wanderings about the dig.

"And what's in here?" Vicky inquired as she raised the corner of a tarpaulin.

"Just tools," Skersh said hurriedly. "Drills and things we use in the digging. You are a very inquisitive young lady." He tried to warm his words with a smile, but Vicky saw the ice in his eyes.

"Yasmin, Hakim," she called. "I'd love to get some pictures of you with all these fascinating things as the background. Pose prettily so I can get you before the light fades," Vicky added. "Oh, and Mr. Skersh, I want a snap of you, too, for my personal scrapbook." She beamed charmingly at Skersh.

"I do not photograph well. And besides, I would look like an ogre beside your pretty friend."

"Oh, come on. Just one shot. Maybe standing here, beside your tent."

"No!" His voice was curt. "But take some of Mademoiselle L-Hassa and her fiancé. Against this dune would be nice." Skersh pointed to a background of sand. In the finished photo it would look like any part of the desert from here to Bagara.

Vicky decided not to argue.

She arranged her camera and began to photograph Yasmin and Hakim, maneuvering them against different backgrounds, attempting to get in all the angles on the dig that she could.

Skersh watched from the side lines. Vicky, her eyes fixed on the view finder, stepped around until she had Skersh's face in focus. There, she had him. She hoped she wasn't too far away to get a good shot of him. Better be sure and take another, she decided.

"Oh, drat," she said. "I've completed this roll. But I have another, and it will only take me a minute to reload. Be patient," she caroled to Yasmin. "I want just another pose or two."

Vicky turned her back to the sun and put her camera under her *chador* to shield out excess light. Her practiced fingers released the film compartment button and extracted the compact roll. She licked the sticking tape and wrapped it securely around the roll.

Suddenly, something struck her shoulder and she lurched forward. The roll dropped from her hands.

Skersh was at her side. "Sorry," he said. "I thought I could help. Oh, you've dropped the roll. Allow me," he said politely and stooped. He fumbled in the sand with great agitation, sputtering apologies. "Ah," he said triumphantly. "Here it is!"

He stood up. The roll of film unfurled like a paper curl, one end of it dangling from his hand.

"Too bad," he shook his head mournfully. "You hadn't yet fastened it against exposure."

But Vicky knew she had.

Vicky looked at him levelly. "I'll simply reload and start from scratch."

"I'm afraid it will not be worth your trouble," he remarked. "See, the desert light fades fast. We must start immediately for the main camp."

Dark shadows were cutting across the dunes.

# 8

# Operation Eavesdrop

HAKIM added his urgings to Yul Skersh's. The whole party would have to ride back to the main camp faster than the leisurely pace of their trip out. They had not come prepared for spending the night on the desert.

"I'll ride lead," Skersh said. "I have a battery lantern with me to light the way. This part of the desert is treacherous with sliding sands. Keep close behind me. I know all the traps and will lead you safely around them."

He spurred his horse to a fast trot. The other three horses caught the rhythm and followed smoothly.

Vicky watched Skersh's light ahead of her, sending out spurts of illumination in time with his horse's gait. No one spoke. Vicky pounded and kneaded together the thoughts which darted into her brain.

Yul Skersh was interested in more than ancient Zourab. He liked its modern aspect—oil. She wished she could have seen those tools more closely. If one of them had been a core drill, she'd have been almost sure of Skersh's real purpose at the dig. A core drill is a vital part of exploring for oil deposits, and hadn't her father told her that Reginald Wilson did not use drills in his excavations? "Too often," he had written to Ken Loring, explaining his work, "valuable clues are lost in hurried digs." Vicky tried to remember what tools she had seen around Wilson's main camp.

Her thoughts centered on Reginald and his wife. A strange couple. And wasn't it peculiar that Reginald Wilson hadn't come to bid them good-by, or safe journey, or something before they'd left. Skersh had said they'd gone to the remote dig at Wilson's suggestion. Funny he didn't come and give the word himself. And she must check Skersh's reason for the absence of workmen at the remote site.

Vicky blinked and shook her head. What was happening to the light? The beam was no longer toward the ground. The shaft of light went straight to the sky, piercing the deep blue. The beam descended and, for a moment, disappeared. Again the beam shot straight up. And disappeared. And again. Was it a signal to the camp to announce the arrival of the party?

A rushing sound swept toward Vicky's ears. The lantern beam picked up dark figures pouring down on the party from either side.

Skersh's horse wheeled and stumbled, sending up a swirl of sand. Vicky signaled "stop" to Yasmin and Hakim, and pulled up her horse. Her heart was pounding, and she didn't know why.

Vicky swiveled around in the saddle and looked about her. Torchlight suddenly surrounded the party of four. In the flickering light, Vicky saw who held the torches. A horde of tribesmen, dirty and mean-looking.

Yasmin and Hakim were pulled from their horses by two of the fierce band. A third was at the bridle of Vicky's horse. She tried to make the horse rear to jerk away. The man held the horse fast and, at the same time, pushed Vicky from the saddle. The tribesman pulled her roughly to her feet and flung her toward Yasmin and Hakim. The three huddled together.

Vicky peered through the unsteady light. Where was Skersh? She could make him out now, being ushered by two more black-robed men to a huge man who sat majestically on a snow-white horse. "He must be the chief," Vicky thought.

"What can all this mean, Hakim?" Vicky whispered. "Do you recognize the tribesmen?"

"I do not," Hakim replied. "They are probably members of what we call a wild tribe, a tribe which does not swear allegiance to the Shah. They refuse to accept his help in any way. They are poor and fierce and vengeful. I fear deep trouble."

Yasmin crept close to Hakim. He put a protective arm around her.

"Do not let them know," he warned, "that you are the daughter of the Shah's Chief Counsel." She shook her head, her eyes wide and frightened.

Vicky kept her eyes on Skersh and the chieftain. The chief's voice sounded menacing. Vicky could not make out the language he used. She indicated to Hakim to translate what was being said. He shrugged his shoulders. "I am afraid I cannot. It is a dialect I do not know," he whispered.

"Skersh is coming back," Vicky reported to her two friends after what seemed like hours. "Perhaps they're going to let us go on."

Skersh came up to them alone. The two men guarding him stayed with the chief.

"He says he is Abdul-Bey, the true ruler of Zourab. He says he will hold us hostages until the Shah recognizes his rights to the kingdom," Skersh said.

"But he will *never* do that," Yasmin breathed. "The chief is mad to think that El Mohama Shah-ja will." Skersh ignored the remark.

"He says we must all accompany him to his encampment. We must do as he says, for now."

Vicky looked around at the warriors. It would be impossible to break for freedom. There were too many of them.

"I guess we don't have any alternative," she said dejectedly. "Perhaps we can think of a way out later."

The guards indicated with a wave of their hands that the four should remount their horses. Immediately, the warriors placed themselves in a square about Hakim, Skersh, Yasmin, and Vicky. Their black figures formed a solid wall around the four, as effective as a dungeon.

The ride to the tribe's encampment was short. They were hurried into one large black goatskin tent. In sign language, the guards told Skersh and Hakim to go to one side, the girls to the other. The guards took up their positions in the center of the tent.

Yasmin crouched near Vicky, shivering. Vicky patted her on the shoulder.

"Don't worry," she said. "We'll find a way out of this mess. Better get some 'closed eye,' as you say." Vicky smiled wanly at the tiny girl and at her own feeble attempt at a joke.

The next morning the camp was alive with sound, animals and children bawling, pots clattering, feet scampering. Vicky got up from her makeshift bed of animal skins. Yasmin was still asleep, and Vicky decided not to disturb her.

Vicky stretched and sauntered toward the tent opening. The one guard on duty watched her go but made no move to stop her.

Yul Skersh was seated outside near a campfire. Two women were apparently serving him something to eat. "He doesn't look very captive to me," Vicky thought. He waved to her to join him.

He motioned to the women. One of them put a steaming cup before Vicky. She sipped it eagerly. The brew was hot and sweet, odd-tasting but welcome.

Skersh leaned toward Vicky. In rapid French he blurted out a fantastic plan for her escape. If she would just get up and race toward the horses, grab one, and flee north, she would make it. Why did she not do this now, and he would take steps to have the others released?

Vicky started to answer him in French. "Your plan is absolute folly," she wanted to say. "There are ten men guarding the horses. Any one of them could stop me. Are you trying to have me killed?"

Instead, she said nothing. She stared blankly into Skersh's face, as if to tell him she hadn't understood. His lips curved into a wise smirk.

"*Eh bien, vous ne le comprenez pas. Les Americains sont bêtes.*" Without another word, he rose and walked away.

"Not so stupid as you think, Monsieur Skersh," Vicky thought wryly to herself. But she was left with uneasy thoughts. The man was as sneaky as a weasel.

Vicky finished the food the women had placed before her. She decided to see how much freedom within the encampment she would be allowed. She walked toward the corral of horses. The guards stopped her. She wandered toward the outskirts of the camp where goats and other animals were tethered. No one seemed to care. A young boy tending the goats smiled at her pleasantly as she stopped to pat a pair of kids.

She wandered back and forth across the whole stretch of the camp. Apparently only the area where the horses were kept was taboo. The answer was simple. The chief was sure they could not escape except by horseback. She began to knit ideas together.

The day dragged on. Yasmin, Hakim, and Vicky strolled restlessly about the camp. They were offered food when mealtime came, but only the serving women came near them. The guards were no longer posted in the tent.

"I wonder where Skersh is," Vicky said in the late afternoon. "He hasn't come near us since midday."

"I saw him over near the horses not long ago," Yasmin reported.

"Really?" Vicky inquired. Interesting. Why was he permitted near the only avenue of escape when she had been kept away?

A few minutes later, Skersh entered the tent where the three were seated. He tossed each of them their saddlebags. "I thought you might want these," he said.

"How kind!" Yasmin said, delighted. "I've yearned for a comb all day."

Vicky picked up her saddlebag thoughtfully. "Very kind," she murmured. "And very fishy, too," she said to herself. He not only was near the horses' corral, but he must have been smack in it to get the bags. Why was he privileged?

But the saddlebags were a blessing. With coins and buttons ripped from her sweater, Vicky made a game of checkers. The "board" was drawn on the back of her writing tablet. Yasmin and Hakim were ready learners, and in no time they were playing almost as professionally as old-time Yankees. Hakim fumed at Yasmin each time she jumped a man.

With the two of them happily engrossed in the game, Vicky devised an activity of her own—trailing Skersh. She spotted him sauntering idly near the goats. Suddenly, he backtracked briskly and started toward the tents set apart from the general encampment—the chief's tents.

Ducking behind the clutter of smaller tents, Vicky kept her eye on Skersh, now heading straight for a big white tent, the only white tent in the whole place. "The chief's! It must be," she decided.

She snatched up a thick rug which lay outside one of the small tents, dropped to all fours and put the rug over her. In a series of short crawls and stops, peering out carefully to make sure no one noticed the traveling, extra-thick carpet, she reached the side of the white tent. She stretched out under the rug, one ear close to the side.

"You have been long in coming to me," the chief of the tribesmen said in badly accented French.

"It was necessary to delay. The three must think me a captive, like them. I cannot do my work in Bagara if I am known to be with you in this undertaking. The American girl is sharp-eyed and sharp-minded."

"What have been your findings?" the chief asked.

Vicky held her breath as she waited for Skersh's reply.

"I am certain I have found the oil. My country is now ready to mount the revolution in your support. Are you prepared?"

"I await the arrival of three chiefs at this camp. Here I shall confer with them and give them their orders."

"Excellent. I must return now," Skersh said. "Have your men take me roughly back to the captives' tent. They must not suspect."

Vicky lay still under the rug. She could hear the sounds of the fake scuffle outside the chief's tent. The tribal dialect's shrill tones bounded through the air. Vicky peered out. Two guards were dragging Skersh away.

Vicky crawled back to the nearest tent and shed her cover. Quickly, she backtracked through the camp by a short route and reached the "jail" tent before Skersh and the two men arrived. She could see him approaching, wrenching away from his captors, screaming condemnations at them—in English, she noted.

Yasmin and Hakim popped out of the tent to view the commotion.

The guards hurled Skersh toward them.

"What happened?" asked Hakim.

"I was caught lurking near the chief's tent. I thought I might be able to see him, perhaps bribe him into letting at least one of us go. I don't really know what I planned to do. I'm just trying desperately to get us out of here."

"Perhaps you'll think of a way yet, Mr. Skersh," Vicky said.

Inwardly, she raged. "The phony! The utter phony!" Well, two could play at this game. She'd try to treat him just as she had before. She'd better not tell Yasmin and Hakim the secret she had overheard. True Zourabians, they'd be sure to show their hatred of their country's enemies. They would be safe only as long as Skersh believed they did not suspect him.

But she knew she *must* escape. She must get back to Bagara—to the Zourab government—to the Shah.

# 9

# The Lucky Accident

VICKY lay stretched out on the animal-skin bed in the captives' tent. Yasmin's steady, soft breathing told Vicky the girl was asleep. But sleep wouldn't come to Vicky. She stared open-eyed at the dark top of the tent. She repeated to herself the exact words she had overheard that afternoon. She must burn them into her memory to report in Bagara. *If* she ever escaped.

"I await the arrival of three chiefs," Abdul-Bey had said. A light gleamed in Vicky's mind.

"There'll be confusion on top of confusion when three more tribes arrive. Perhaps I'll find a way to escape in the midst of the hubbub."

The hopeful thought relaxed her enough to let her drift off to sleep.

Two days wearily came and went. Nothing happened. The checker game became a bore.

In the evening of the second day, as Vicky wandered aimlessly about, she saw a great cloud of sand whirling toward the camp. Excitement rose in her.

"The expected chieftains must be arriving," she said half aloud. "Now perhaps I can go into action."

The arrival set up a great clamor. Men, women, children, animals swarmed in like a cattle stampede.

Should she act boldly? Now? Try to grab one of the several horses being held by that small boy over there? She started toward him.

Suddenly, Skersh was at her side. And two guards were with him. One of the guards seized Vicky's arm.

"They fear in the confusion one of us might plan to escape," Skersh explained. "They are ordering us back to our tent. We have no alternative."

Vicky wrenched herself free from the guard's grasp. Furious because her high hopes had been smashed, she shouted angrily, "I'll go back under my own steam."

The guard didn't understand a word, but the fury in her voice held him back. He didn't grab at her, but let her stamp away toward the tent.

"Bravo," Skersh said snidely.

The whole episode left Vicky trembling with determination. She'd escape if only to show Skersh she could.

The free space around the captives' tent was now crowded with women and children. Piles of rugs and household goods blocked Vicky's way. Directly in front of the jail tent, a new family had set up housekeeping. Vicky stepped carefully over their possessions and sat down outside the flap of her tent.

The toddler member of the nomad family waddled unsteadily about. The long robe he was wearing tripped him and he fell toward the cooking fire his mother had just lighted. One flowing sleeve was licked with flame.

In a darting movement, Vicky snatched up her *chador* and ran to him. She wrapped it around the child's arm, extinguishing the flame. The toddler howled in fright and panic.

Vicky unwound the scorched *chador* and picked off the burned pieces of cloth from the child's arm. Fortunately the sleeve had been of thickly padded cloth. The little arm was warm to her touch as she examined it, but not burned. Instinctively, she held the little one against her shoulder and comforted him. The cries turned to whimperings.

Vicky brought out her pocket flash and gave it to him to hold. The baby gurgled in delight as she flashed the tiny light on and off.

The child's mother, coming back to the camp, dropped the two water bags she carried. She snatched the child and held him tightly to her breast. She examined the burned sleeve and the child's arm. Her liquid brown eyes looked questioningly at Vicky. Then she spotted Vicky's burned *chador*. She made gestures as if to say, "You saved him, did you not? You saved my little boy."

Vicky nodded her head. The woman smiled and murmured something in a warm tone. Vicky realized she must be thanking her.

The woman picked up the burned *chador*, looked at it, shook her head sadly and threw the *chador* to one side. Then she rummaged into a pile of goods and brought out a long blue robe exactly like the one she herself wore. She unfolded it and held it out toward Vicky.

Vicky shook her head. "No. My *chador* can be replaced. It is nothing." She patted the child's head to indicate that the important thing was the child's welfare.

The woman persisted, taking Vicky's arm and laying the robe across it.

Bang! The idea came to Vicky like a shot. The nomads would be moving on after the chief's pow-wow, wouldn't they!

"You've just handed me the key to my cell," Vicky thought.

She jumped up and gave the woman a big hug. She knew now what she was going to do. She'd better tell Yasmin and Hakim her plan.

"So, all I have to do is watch the family for signs that they're leaving camp. With this robe, I'll look just like one of them. I'll slip out with the tribe. When we're far enough away from here, I'll try to get back to Mazzun."

Vicky sat back on her heels and waited for Hakim and Yasmin's reaction. The whispered conference was taking place around the checkerboard in the light of a tiny oil lamp.

Yasmin's amber eyes were cloudy.

"It is so very dangerous. Suppose a guard catches you?" she asked.

"I'll see to it that he doesn't," Vicky replied determinedly.

"The desert is treacherous for one who does not know it," Hakim pointed out. He paused. "But I have a compass in my saddlebag. You are quick to learn.

I will teach you as much as I can of this area before you leave."

"Hakim," Yasmin hissed angrily. "Surely you are not encouraging her to go!"

"I must, my little one, it is our only chance," he said softly.

"Only one of us can go, don't you see?" Vicky urged. "That's why you can't even tell Skersh. He might try to stop me, and I'm really the only one who has a chance to escape and get help. I have the confidence of this nomad mother. I do not believe she will give me away even if she recognizes me. Hakim must stay here to protect *you*."

"The plan is bold," Yasmin said slowly. She smiled in the gloom. "And you are very O.K. to even try it. May the eye of Allah be upon you and see you to safety," she added with grave sincerity.

All that evening, Skersh was away from the captives' tent. "The big deal must be going on," Vicky figured to herself. "And he's probably in on the whole thing. I wonder how he'll explain away his absence for all this time."

The next morning, Vicky spent some time amusing the children of her newly adopted "family." Using sign language and smiles, she found she could communicate very nicely with them.

In the middle of the morning, the mother of the family started giving orders to her children. Clapping her hands impatiently, scolding them, pointing out tasks for them to do, she got the group organized for packing.

Vicky couldn't help but think, "She's just like Aunt Ellen getting Dad and me ready for a trip. No mistake who's in charge here."

Vicky slipped away from the group and into the jail tent. Skersh was not there. First, she tied to the belt of her riding pants the small canteen she had carried in her saddlebag. She'd had it since childhood camping days. She patted it. "It's come a long way from the Maine woods," she thought.

On the other hip, she fastened a small packet of food that had been carefully saved by all three. With Yasmin's help she put on the concealing robe. Hakim pointed out her riding boots.

"They'll give you away," he said. "Better hide them some way."

"Wait," Yasmin said, "I know a way to do it." She rummaged in her saddlebag and pulled out a *zada*. Swiftly, she tore the colorful scarf into strips and soiled them with dirt from the tent floor. Then she skillfully wrapped them around Vicky's boots.

"A perfect camouflage," Vicky approved. "They look

just like the ragged cloth these women bind on their feet. Now, give me the compass and I'm off."

Without a sound, she slipped out of the tent, grabbed a knotted bundle and hoisted it over her shoulder. She joined the trail of women following their men out of the camp.

# 10

## Kajar Mansur

VICKY moved along slowly behind the mother of her
adopted family. She kept as close to her as possible,
not only because she thought it safer, but also because
it was comforting. These people, at least, liked her.
The bundle on her back was heavy and the sun was
hot, but she scarcely felt it.

"But I'm out! I'm away!" her heart said. She dared
not look back to see if the wild tribe's camp was out
of sight.

On and on she trudged through the heat and the
heavy sand, each step taking her farther and farther
away and, she hoped, nearer and nearer to Mazzun.

111

She hoped they'd never stop. Stopping might bring discovery.

The line of people was slowing down. Vicky hunched herself into the robe and pulled its hood ever further over her face. The women were shifting positions. Those who had been on the horses and camels dismounted. Walking women mounted them.

"So that's the system," Vicky thought. "If I can just get my chance at a horse!"

A tap on her shoulder made her jump. She turned her almost completely hooded face around. The mother of the child she had saved took Vicky's hand and led her to a horse. Vicky mounted as best she could, trying not to show any of the clothes she wore beneath the robe. The mother placed the child on a soft bundle in front of Vicky. Vicky put her arms around him. The child twisted around, his little fingers grabbing at the protecting hood. The mother peered up at Vicky.

"She knows!" Vicky thought wildly.

The woman's brown eyes lighted up. She nodded her head in recognition and put one finger to her lips, then against her heart.

Vicky heaved a sigh of relief. The woman was going to keep her secret. But she knew now she could never make her escape on horseback while she held the nomad child. She would have to wait for another time, and get away as best she could on foot.

Just before the midday stop, Vicky took out the compass Hakim had given her. She swallowed nervously. They weren't heading toward Mazzun at all! They were heading away from it, in a direction Hakim had told her was nothing but mountains inhabited by the wild tribes. She'd have to leave the nomads and strike out on her own. The thought chilled her to the bone.

In the bustle of the stop, Vicky walked to the outskirts of the group. When they left, she would slip behind the huge dune she had marked with her eye and let them pass on ahead.

The nomads began to make the motions of starting their trek once again. Vicky slowed her pace and let several groups pass her.

She felt a quick tug at her arm. A hand held out a goatskin sack and pushed it at Vicky. The woman walked on ahead rapidly. Hanging from her back, papoose-style, was the toddler.

The whole group passed by as Vicky stood looking at the disappearing back of the woman who had befriended her.

Almost jauntily, Vicky started off in the direction her compass told her was the way to Mazzun. When the nomads were well out of sight, she sat in the shadow of a dune and opened the goatskin sack. In it was a smaller sack filled with water, a chunk of soft, white cheese wrapped in a thin piece of hide, and some flat bread.

Vicky ate with relish, but stopped short of her hunger. "I'd better ration myself, even though this windfall adds to the supply I brought." She repacked the food and arranged it once again under her robe. She checked her compass and started out across the endless sand.

The sun beat down mercilessly on her and she removed the heavy blue robe. The relief was only momentary. Whirling sand stung her face and shoulders. She put it on once more.

Hour after hour she plodded on. Toward evening, before the light failed, she climbed a high dune to look about her. The steep climb was exhausting. She lay on top of the mound, breathing heavily, her lungs screaming for air.

She dragged herself wearily to a standing position and looked about her. In the distance, she could see black dots. She could not tell if they were moving or not. A camel train? Another band of nomads? She would head toward the dots, anyhow, whatever they were. Anything was better than the bitter loneliness of the vast desert.

She started down the dune. The goatskin sack broke loose from her belt. She tripped over it and went hurtling down, down the hill of sand. She rolled to a stop, tried to stagger to her feet, but pitched forward, unconscious.

"Mmmmm," Vicky murmured in delight. The mist of the waterfall she was standing in swirled about her, cool, cool, cool. She lifted her face to the sparkling trickle and began to drink the marvelous liquid which danced down her throat.

She opened her eyes and the beautiful waterfall faded away.

In panic, she pushed with all her strength against what she saw was a man who held her cradled easily in one arm.

"Now, now," he said soothingly. "It is all right. You are safe. Rest."

Vicky sank back against his arm and gazed at him. She must still be dreaming. "I must be in a movie," her whizzing brain told her.

The face of the young man was tanned, lean, and smooth. His large brown eyes were flecked with golden lights. His well-chiseled mouth was smiling reassuringly at her. The protective desert cloak he wore was of soft, white linen. He had thrown back the hood, but it still framed his handsome face and his black shining hair.

"Do not speak for a while," he said. "Rest. I am Kajar Mansur, Khan of the Shiram-Zi. We shall go soon to my people who will take care of you."

Vicky closed her eyes and popped them open once more. The Khan of the Shiram-Zi was still there. She wasn't dreaming any more.

"Here. One more sip of water and we shall be on our way." Gracefully he raised a silver canteen to Vicky's lips and cautioned, "One sip only."

Vicky drank dutifully and started to rise to her feet. She wobbled unsteadily.

"No, you are too weak. Allow me." The young man lifted Vicky in two strong arms and sat her on his horse. He sprang to the saddle behind her, keeping one protective arm about her. The horse answered his touch and moved sure-footedly off through the desert.

Vicky leaned against his arm and heaved a sigh. For the time being, it was bliss to be taken care of. "The eye of Allah was certainly upon me," she thought, remembering Yasmin's words. "Perhaps now I can get to Bagara to warn the Shah—and get help for the others."

"Ho!" Kajar Mansur boomed as they rode into the camp. Two men came quickly to him and held his horse. Kajar swung out of the saddle and lifted Vicky down. "Steady," he said. "Try your legs a bit."

He supported Vicky as she wobbled about getting the circulation back into her limbs.

"Call my mother and her women," ordered Kajar. The two servants scurried away.

Kajar took Vicky to a tent and gently led her in. The tent was festooned with gay, hand-woven banners on the sides. Bright rugs, silky-looking and deep, were spread on the floor. Large, soft cushions were thrown in profusion about them. Gratefully, Vicky sank down on one of them.

"My mother will be here soon to tend you," he announced and left the tent.

Vicky didn't hear his last words. She was already asleep.

Vicky woke with a start. Then her eyes focused on the bright banners and the soft rugs and she remembered where she was. The tent of Kajar Mansur was lamplit now. Night must have come while she slept. Beside her sat a small woman. Her face crinkled into a smile and she laid a cool hand on Vicky's forehead.

"You are awake, little one, and you are not feverish. Come, you shall bathe and refresh yourself," she said decisively. Her hands clapped in two short bursts and two women scuttled into the room with a large basin, perfume, water, and clothing.

"I feel like a new person," Vicky announced to the women when she had finished bathing and changing. The women nodded and smiled and hurried out, taking Vicky's soiled clothing with them.

Vicky looked herself over carefully. She wore an embroidered turquoise silk robe, colorful and comfortable. Her feet were encased in slippers heavily embroidered with gold thread. The women had brushed her dark curls until they gleamed.

Kajar Mansur entered the tent.

"Ah, ah! The desert bundle I found has turned into a beautiful young lady," he said approvingly. "You must be hungry. We shall eat in my mother's tent." He bowed low and led her out with a sweeping flourish of his hand.

The low table was covered with a fine linen cloth. It was sumptuous with roasted partridge, rice, eggplant, yogurt, and mounds of sliced melon. Silver dishes held other fruits and nuts. A flickering oil lamp hung from a chain overhead.

Halfway through the delectable meal, Vicky remembered her manners. Why, she hadn't even identified herself to these kind people! And they had been too polite to ask.

"Forgive me," she began, "for not explaining myself to you. My name is Victoria Loring." The words flowed out, about her father, her job, the reasons for being in Zourab.

Kajar and his mother listened with interest.

"Although I have never been in your country, I have read much about it. From your boots and canteen I surmised you were an American. I had hoped to go to the United States after completing my education in Paris and in London. Events in Zourab called me back to my homeland, however."

"Events?" Vicky questioned.

"We are an old country," Kajar began to explain, "and many of our tribal ways remain the same. But the new discoveries of our vast oil fields have forced us to become modern with great haste. I am Khan—or chief—of my tribe, and rule all the Shiram-Zi. There are others like me in other tribes. We rule our own people but are loyal to El Mohama Shah-ja. He sees to it that the wealth pouring in from the oil is used for the good of all the people, not just for the benefit of a few tribes."

"I know," Vicky put in.

Kajar's handsome face clouded over. "There are a few mountain tribes—wild ones—who seek to gather the oil money for themselves. They claim Mohama is not the true ruler. I have come home to offer my allegiance once again to the Shah."

Wheels began to turn in Vicky's head. The loyal tribes, then, did not know that the wild ones were getting outside help. Kajar Mansur thought the tribal unrest was entirely native.

Vicky weighed her thoughts carefully. Should the information she had be given only to the Shah? Could she trust Kajar with her knowledge? She decided he must know.

Vicky leaned forward. "Listen," she said. "I have many things to tell you."

She sketched rapidly for him the visit to the dig, the capture, the overheard interview between Abdul-Bey and Skersh. She told him how she had escaped in an attempt to warn the Shah and get help for her friends. Kajar followed her every word. He did not interrupt once.

At the end of Vicky's story he rose and paced back and forth in the tent.

At last Kajar said, "Yes. You are right. I do not think you need fear, at the moment, for the safety of your friends. This Skersh still feels secure. He probably does not even worry himself about your escape, thinking you would perish alone in the desert. That gives us time—time to get to the Shah."

Kajar's mother and Vicky followed his every movement as he paced up and down.

"The wild tribes, by themselves, would not be a serious danger," he continued. "With guns and money from the enemy country to the north, they would be a terrible threat to Zourab. Worse than that. The tribes are uneducated, primitive. It would be easy to twist and bend them if they ever seized the throne. Our enemy must know this." He slammed his fist into his palm.

"Can you get me to Bagara?" Vicky asked. "I can warn the government and . . ."

"Yes, yes, that's it. You go to the Shah, and I shall speed to the loyal tribes and get their help to prevent this evil plot." Solemnly, he looked at Vicky. "Zourab will never forget its pretty American savior."

He turned to his mother and spoke rapidly in the tribe's language. His mother left immediately and was back in an instant. She placed before Vicky a thick, silky rug, the most beautiful Vicky had ever seen.

Kajar explained. "It is yours. It is your Shiram-Zi home, for we say 'Where my carpet is, there is my home.' My mother has officially welcomed you into our tribe."

Vicky took the woman's hands in hers. "I shall try," she said, "to be a worthy daughter of the Shiram-Zi."

# 11

## Jalboot to Bagara

"THE ride will be hard and fast," Kajar warned Vicky as they prepared to leave the camp at dawn the next morning. "To save the most time, I shall take you to the seacoast. There you can take a boat to the capital."

"I'll keep up with you," Vicky promised. "Just take me the shortest way."

Kajar moved quickly once his decision was made. Vicky changed back into her riding clothes in a hurry. Fresh, lively horses were saddled and the two galloped out of camp in the growing light.

Kajar knew his way about his country. Without seeming to use any direction-finder, he cut across the desert and found a well-worn trail through land studded with rocks and scrub vegetation. He alternated the pace so that neither the horses nor the riders would tire. By sunup they were far from the camp.

During one of the leisurely moments on the trail, Vicky had a chance to study the handsome young man. "He must be about Jeff's age," she thought, "but he seems so much older, so much more mature."

She laughed softly. Wouldn't Jeff writhe when she described Kajar to him and made that observation! Jeff was so sure he was the complete man-of-the-world and Vicky not much more than a curly-headed kid.

"I wonder how he'd like this whole scene," she mused. "Here I am, galloping along with the handsomest Khan in captivity . . . and hot on one of the biggest stories yet. He'd probably be livid if he knew." She wondered which would make him more jealous— her being with this man, or having the big story? She'd ask him when she saw him again. He'd probably come out with some horrible pun like "I really khan-not say."

Vicky giggled at the thought.

Kajar drew his horse up. "There, ahead." He pointed down the trail.

Vicky could just see a flash of sunlight on water. They were almost at the coast of the gulf.

In a very short time, they had ridden into a small town which seemed to be stuck like a tarnished pin on the coastline. There were a few small, poor-looking houses, drab in color and without the typical Zourab ornamentation.

The dock, however, was large and well-constructed. Small boats with oddly shaped, roughly triangular sails, their prows graceful points, dotted the waters of the gulf. "This is but a fishing village," Kajar said. "The small *dhows* you see do not make long trips. I am hunting the owner of that large boat, over there," he pointed out. "It is a *jalboot*—a coastal *dhow*—and it has an engine."

Kajar strode along the dock which was lined on either side with piles of kegs, boxes, and ropes. Vicky walked fast beside him to keep up.

"It will be difficult to convince the captain you must go aboard. *Jalboot* captains are superstitious about women aboard," Kajar said. "Luckily, I know him. The Shiram-Zi spend the winter months along the coast and travel to the mountains only when spring comes.

"Wait here," he added, "while I go and try to bargain with him."

At the sight of Kajar, the captain leaped from the deck of the *jalboot* to the dock shouting a greeting and waving his arms with flourishing gestures. As Kajar talked to him, the man began to shake his head fiercely, pull at his hair dramatically, stamp his foot. Kajar's quiet voice continued through the emotional performance. The man finally simmered down.

Kajar motioned Vicky to come ahead. Vicky walked up to the man, her gift carpet folded conspicuously over one arm.

"See," Kajar explained. "She is a true Shiram-Zi. Where her carpet is, there is her home. She will not truly be on your *jalboot*, but in her own home. You need not fear the spirits of the water. Your boat will come to no harm."

The man thought this over carefully. Finally, he jumped aboard his boat.

Vicky sensed the time to act was now. She clambered over the ship's rail, spread her carpet out, and sat cross-legged on it.

"Good," Kajar said. "On the trip, do not move about unless you carry the carpet. Otherwise our good friend the captain will tremble in fear of the wrath of the water goblins."

"Oh, I shall. The carpet will keep the goblins of fear away from my head, too. It will remind me of a lovely mother—and her charming son," Vicky said.

Kajar's glorious smile flashed at the compliment.

"Your journey will not be too long. And I rather think our captain friend will open his motor wide and set a record. Shiram-Zi carpet or no, he won't want to test the temper of the water spirits any longer than necessary."

The captain was already starting his engine. It coughed twice, and then settled down to a rhythmic whirr.

"Here," Kajar said hurriedly. "Take this ring. Give it to the Shah as a symbol of my allegiance. Tell him I am on my way to the chieftains of all the loyal tribes."

The boat captain had already loosened his *jalboot* from the mooring. The craft began to move away from the dock.

Vicky stood in the bow of the boat, the carpet soft beneath her feet, and waved until Kajar was out of sight.

Once outside the harbor beyond the fishing *dhows*, the *jalboot* suddenly picked up speed, almost knocking Vicky to the deck.

"The captain's determined to get rid of his cargo in nothing flat," she said.

She sat cross-legged on her carpet and examined the ring Kajar had given her. It was studded with blue-green stones set in gold, and the shape . . . "Why the shape is almost like the button I found in the bazaar!"

A flood of all the events of the past week poured into Vicky's mind. She had a lot of things to do in Bagara.

"And I must look up Pamela Wilson. You know," she thought to herself, "I never did tell her I found one of her golden buttons."

# 12

## The Busy M. Najeeb

THE fairy-tale towers of Bagara cast shimmering reflections among a thousand fishing boats as the jalboot cut across the harbor in the rays of the setting sun. Finally, amid a forest of masts and furled sails, Vicky saw a long dock on which some fishermen were mending nets. The *jalboot* captain was making for it and Vicky, clutching her carpet, stood up and moved to the rail. With sweeping gestures the captain indicated that she was to get out of his boat the moment it touched the dock.

"Don't worry," Vicky said. "I'm as anxious to leave, friend, as you are to have me go."

The *jalboot* bumped against the pilings and Vicky hopped out. The boat backed out immediately and headed for open water.

"He's probably going straight back to erase his own wake so the goblins won't ever know what happened. Good luck to him."

Amid the curious stares of the fishermen, Vicky ran from the dock and plunged into the whirlpool of the crowded streets of Bagara. It was a section of the city she had not toured, and it seemed strange and a little frightening to her. She hugged her carpet close and hurried on. She could see the onion-domed government ministry in the distance. If she could reach there, she'd know her way back to the hotel. She plunged on, battling her way through the people and the slow ox carts, and dodging cars and taxis being driven wildly by devil-may-care Zourabians.

The bazaar where she and Yasmin had shopped suddenly appeared on her right. Cheers! She knew now how near she was to the hotel.

The clerk at the hotel was overcome with excitement when she asked for the key to her room.

"Mademoiselle," he screamed. "You are here! Safe! And the others? Stay right here. Stay right here until I get the manager." He danced off backwards, making "stay put" motions with his hands.

The manager appeared, full of smiles and bows and rattling off explanations.

Vicky learned that Reginald Wilson had reported their absence from the dig. Her father and Monsieur L-Hassa had left Bagara immediately with a search party.

"They have been gone several days and I have no word from them," he added, breathless from his message.

"Is any one from my father's camera crew in the hotel?" Vicky asked.

"No, the camera men are gone, too. They left with your father."

Vicky pondered the situation as she went to her room. What was the next step to take? How could she get to the Shah without Monsieur L-Hassa's help?

A thought struck her. "Of course! I'll go to Yasmin's father's secretary. Najeeb ought to be able to help me. It's too late to reach him today—but I'll get to him first thing in the morning."

Early the next morning, she entered the ministry building. "I just hope Najeeb is here Where will I turn if he isn't?"

Najeeb was in, all right, and haranguing someone over the telephone. As Vicky approached the desk,

Najeeb's jaw dropped in surprise. He replaced the phone receiver, his eyes wide with disbelief.

"You . . . you . . ." he mumbled in confusion, "esc. . ." He bit off the word.

"Yes, me," Vicky said sharply. "He was going to say 'escaped,' I'm sure of it," she thought to herself. "How does he know I was ever captured? This man is as slick as oil," she decided. But she'd need his help in getting to the Shah. She would have to be cagey.

Najeeb covered his confusion with a low bow and flowery greetings.

"Ah! Monsieur L-Hassa's search has been successful. You have all been found. But why are you here alone? Why are the others not with you?"

Vicky thought fast. Best not to reveal anything to him. "The rest of the party is still at Mazzun. I have come in alone with a message from Monsieur L-Hassa. He wants me to see the Shah. In person. He says you are to make all the necessary arrangements for me to see him immediately."

Najeeb's eyes narrowed cunningly. "The Shah has left on his holy pilgrimage. He will not return for three days. For three days he will fast and pray and will not speak with anyone," he said. "Surely Monsieur L-Hassa knows this is the time of the year that the Shah makes his pilgrimage."

It was Vicky's turn to be confused. "Drat, he's seen through my trick," she thought. "I'll have to get to the dig and find out where Dad has gone hunting for me. Monsieur L-Hassa *must* have my story."

She suddenly remembered what Reginald Wilson had told her. *The dig gets in touch with Najeeb if they need supplies.* Perhaps Najeeb could make contact with the dig.

"Can you get me in touch with Mr. Wilson or Mrs. Wilson at the dig?" Vicky demanded. "By shortwave," she added, to show the man that she knew of their regular communications.

"Alas, I cannot. I can only speak with the dig when they signal our operator here in Bagara. Unfortunately, I have heard nothing from Mr. Wilson in many days. His wife, poor lady, still remains in jail. He has not even inquired for her."

"Mrs. Wilson's still in jail?" Vicky asked, astonished. "But Monsieur L-Hassa assured me the mistake had been corrected! Yasmin and I assured Pamela Wilson she would be freed. Why wasn't this done? Why is she still in jail?"

Najeeb shrugged his shoulders. "Perhaps Monsieur L-Hassa neglected to give the order for her release. It would be out of place for me to question him, and it is not in my power to release her."

"Well, may I see Mrs. Wilson?" Vicky asked. "Perhaps Pamela," she thought to herself, "can tell me how to get transportation to the dig, or to Mazzun, at least."

"I am sorry. It is not in my power to give you a pass to the jailer. I am so very sorry." Najeeb held his palms upward to show how humbly he regretted having to tell her this.

"Why not?" Vicky insisted. "Surely as the secretary to the Chief Counsel of the Shah you have some authority."

Najeeb simply smirked at her and shrugged once again. He smoothed his enormous mustache, shuffled some papers on his desk, selected one, and started to read. "I am a busy man," he said. "Excuse me, but I have work to do."

Utterly frustrated, Vicky turned and stamped out of the ministry building. She'd have to make other plans.

Still angry, Vicky walked briskly along the streets toward her hotel. All at once, she was aware of rapid footsteps behind her. She swung about. A white-robed figure passed rapidly by her. She could not see the man's face, but she couldn't help thinking of the face she had seen in the jail window.

"I'm jumpy as a scared cat," she admitted to herself. "The man's probably just on his way to the bazaar."

She wondered if she should try to see Pamela Wilson anyhow. Perhaps she could persuade the jailer to let her in. She started toward the jail and changed her mind. "Now, wait a minute," she said. "That wouldn't do any good at all. What you have to do is get to Dad, and Yasmin's father."

She turned back in the direction of the hotel. "I'll be able to hire a car and a driver there and head out to the dig." She hurried along, feeling better now that she had a definite plan in mind.

She picked up her key at the hotel desk. "No," the clerk said in answer to her question, "there has been no word from the party in the desert."

Vicky fitted the key into the lock and clicked open the door.

"Oooh," she cried as she looked about her. The room was a shambles. Clothing from the drawers of the bureau was scattered everywhere. The bedding had been torn from the bed. The pillows were slashed. Feathers were everywhere.

"What on earth were they after?" Vicky said aloud. The quick check she made showed her that nothing had actually been taken from the room. "What *were* they after?"

The puzzled frown on her face was wiped away by the light dawning in her mind.

"The button!" she gasped. "I'll bet someone was after the button."

Vicky dashed to the bathroom. Her traveling cosmetic case lay on a bench covered by the towel she had carelessly flung on it that morning. She rummaged in it for the jar of cold cream. Feeling carefully through the thick cream, her fingers closed on the golden object. She pulled out the coated button.

"I don't know why I hid this thing," she said to herself. "But I'm awfully glad I did. But why, just why is this darned button so important to someone?"

She washed the button off, wrapped it in tissue, and put it in her pocket with the ring Kajar had given her for the Shah.

A knock sounded at the door.

"Who is there?" she asked. She was amazed to find that her voice trembled.

"Mademoiselle," the voice said. "Your father is on the phone in the manager's office."

Vicky's heart gave a glad leap. She tore over to the door, flung it open, and was halfway down the stairs before the startled messenger could say anything more.

"Dad!" Vicky shouted into the phone. "Oh, am I glad to hear from you!"

"Vicky, darling, are you all right? I've been frantic with worry. . . ."

"Dad, where are you? I've too much to tell you. I can't do it on the phone. Where are you? And I'll get there as fast as possible!" Vicky said in a rush.

"We're at Mazzun—at least our headquarters are here. We've been everywhere looking for you. Is Yas . . . .?"

"Don't go away. I'll get out to you as fast as a jeep can take me." Vicky slammed the receiver down.

"Can you get me a jeep and a trustworthy driver?" she asked the hotel manager. "And fast," she ordered.

# 13

## Mountain Hop

"Faster, faster," Vicky urged.

Vicky clung tightly to the side of the jeep, bracing herself against its jolting as they bounced over the rough road.

"I just hope he knows what he's doing and where he's going." The words jumped around in Vicky's head. "This isn't the road Hakim took. I just hope this driver is right when he says it's a short cut. And I wish he'd cut that infernal racket."

The driver had kept up a steady tune as he drove, a high tinny wail, punctuated by grunts as the jeep bumped over ruts.

Vicky kept her eyes straight ahead, hunting for something familiar which would tell her they were nearing Mazzun. There! Those were palms up ahead. They were coming into Mazzun.

"You're a doll after all," she said to the singing driver. "I take back everything I've been thinking about you."

The driver stopped his wailing song long enough to grin.

"You didn't understand a single word, did you?" Vicky said. "But you like the way I said it." She smiled back at the man in a friendly fashion.

The jeep swung into the oasis town.

"Now, where to find Dad?" The only place she knew was the eating pavilion where Yasmin, Hakim, and she had lunched—how many ages ago? She'd go there. Someone was bound to know where a dignitary like M. L-Hassa had his headquarters.

She poked the driver and pointed her finger in the direction she wanted him to take. He nodded his head and obeyed.

The jeep drew up in front of the café. Vicky spotted Ken Loring pacing restlessly up and down in front of it, his face drawn with worry.

"Dad!" She was out of the jeep in one leap and into her father's arms.

"Baby, are you all right? You're not hurt or anything?" Ken Loring looked his daughter over carefully. "Where are Yasmin and Hakim? And what's *happened?*" he blurted out.

"Where's Monsieur L-Hassa, Dad?" Vicky asked excitedly. "He's got to hear the whole story—and it's a weird one."

"We'll go to him now. We're camped on the outskirts of Mazzun. We've been traveling out into the desert each day, sending search parties in every direction, trying to find you. I've horses waiting. Can you make the trek now?"

"Absolutely. We musn't waste a minute," Vicky answered decisively.

During the ride to the camp, Vicky reconstructed the whole story in her mind. "It's almost unbelievable," she decided.

Monsieur L-Hassa greeted her warmly, trying to hide the anxiety in his eyes. "What of Yasmin?" he asked.

Vicky began at the beginning. As the incredible tale unfolded, the two men's faces were swept with astonishment. Neither man interrupted her during the story.

"So, you see," Vicky finished, "capturing Yasmin, Hakim, and me was another ace up Skersh's sleeve. With us as hostages he could always get through to you, Monsieur L-Hassa, and so bring even more pressure to bear on the Shah. But I'm almost certain no harm has come to Yasmin and Hakim. Skersh has been pretending—and my guess is he *still* is—that he is a captive also. I did not tell Yasmin and Hakim of the plot I overheard."

"But where can they be found? We have combed the desert for all of you," Ken Loring said. "We never spotted any wild tribe."

"I know one man who could probably find them," Vicky answered. "Kajar Mansur. But I do not know where to find him. All I know is that he was going to visit all the loyal tribe leaders and rally them to the Shah's support. He could be anywhere," she finished with a sigh.

"Did he say how he was going to make his tour of the tribes?" Monsieur L-Hassa said intently.

"No, no he didn't. Why do you ask?" Vicky questioned.

"Kajar Mansur is a skilled pilot. He flies his own plane, equipped with special wheels which he himself designed that enable him to make landings and take-offs on the desert sand."

"His plane!" Vicky exploded. "But he was traveling like a nomad, on horseback, with tents. . . ." she finished lamely. Her imagination conjured up the picture of the feast in Kajar's mother's tent—the pillows, the rugs, the silver dishes. It had all seemed so exotic, so Zourabian. It was hard to see Kajar in anything but desert surroundings.

M. L-Hassa seemed not to have heard Vicky's words. He was thoughtfully pacing up and down. "There's a chance," he said, "a very *good* chance, that we can reach Kajar Mansur quickly. When flying, he is in constant communication with the tower at the Bagara airport. In our small country, he is hardly ever out of radio range. I'll dispatch a fast horse and rider to Mazzun to telephone Najeeb. Najeeb can inform the tower, which in turn can summon Kajar and ask him to meet us here."

"Najeeb," Vicky thought. "Could he be trusted to do anything?" Aloud she said, "I saw Najeeb before I left Bagara. I did not mention this before," she added, "but he told me that Pamela Wilson is still in custody. Why, Monsieur L-Hassa?"

"What?" he said, outraged. "I can not believe it! Najeeb was given orders to arrange her release. The British Consulate was informed by me that this had been done. I cannot understand what could have happened. Najeeb will answer to me for this. . . ." Angrily, M. L-Hassa strode out to send the rider to a telephone in Mazzun.

Minutes, an hour, another hour dragged by. Vicky, her father, and Yasmin's father paced nervously about the tent. Yes, the rider had relayed the message to Najeeb. Yes, Najeeb had said he would do exactly as commanded. But had he? Had he? Vicky couldn't keep the needling question out of her mind. She was sure the slippery secretary couldn't be trusted.

Suddenly, excited cries rang through the air outside the tent. Shouts and wild whoops sounded. Vicky and the two men rushed to the opening of the tent to see what was causing the commotion.

"*Avion! Avion!*" Vicky made out the French word. "A plane!" the camp servants were shouting.

Vicky saw the small plane circle over the encampment and swing in for a landing several hundred feet away.

The plane hit the ground, sending up a spray of sand, and rolled to a stop. The pilot climbed out of the cockpit and walked briskly in their direction.

"Kajar!" Vicky shouted as she ran toward him.

"My little lost friend," Kajar greeted her gaily. "I looked for you in Bagara; I am happy to find you here."

Vicky linked her arm in his and the two walked briskly back to Ken Loring and Aba L-Hassa. "You're a heaven-sent gift," Vicky bubbled. "Thank goodness you could get here."

Words, ideas, plans flew through the air as the three men and Vicky talked. The decisions were quickly made. Vicky and her father would go with Kajar to hunt out the wild tribes' mountain hide-out and rescue Yasmin and Hakim. Monsieur L-Hassa would go back to Bagara, interrupt the Shah's three-day holy retreat, warn him of the revolutionary threat, and prepare to greet the loyal chieftains who were now converging on the capital to offer him their allegiance.

"May Allah's finger point the way to my daughter for you," Monsieur L-Hassa said at the end. "I wish with all my heart I could go with you. But the Shah must know Miss Loring's message."

He turned to Vicky. "You are a remarkably brave girl," he said. "The Shah shall know of your contribution to our country's welfare."

The neat little plane, Vicky was pleased to discover, was carpeted in Shiram-Zi style, the rugs a duplicate in design of the one she had been given. Kajar carried his home in the skies.

She was delighted, too, at the way her father and Kajar seemed to get on together. Kajar asked intelligent questions about Ken Loring's work and the documentary. "It will be good for the world to know the truth about us," he said.

Vicky was only half-conscious of the conversation. She was seated at the plane's window with Kajar's powerful binoculars glued to her eyes, watching with tense fascination as the landscape of Zourab slipped by.

The terrain beneath the plane was no longer sandy desert. She looked down on brown mountains, jagged and rocky, with very little vegetation and apparently no life.

The rugged terrain below seemed to resent the plane's smooth flight. Without warning, downdrafts reached up like rough arms and jerked the plane toward the rocky earth below. Jetting updrafts wrested the small plane from their grasp and tossed it skyward like a toy balloon.

"Seat belts," Kajar called out as he wrestled with the wheel. "Fasten them quickly. It is rugged flying here."

"You're so right," Vicky shouted to him. The binoculars she had been using had slipped from her eyes and rammed into her face as she was tilted sideways. She put them down and clumsily fastened her belt as she was jolted roughly from one side of the little plane to the other.

The plane was being tossed about like a leaf in a hurricane, but they flew on and on. The buffeting churned Vicky's stomach to a froth. She gulped repeatedly, fighting the queasy stomach. She was determined not to be airsick. Not now, of all times. Not when she'd never been before. She looked at her father.

Ken Loring, sitting very quietly, had turned a sickly white shade.

Only Kajar seemed immune. Seeing his passengers' plight, he put his plane in a steep climb. In a few minutes they had risen above the turbulence and the flight became smoother.

Vicky drew a deep breath and resumed her spotting job. She scanned the rugged cliffs through the glasses. The plane was skimming over the mountain peaks. It seemed to Vicky that they were almost brushing them. She concentrated as hard as she could to look past the scenery.

Suddenly, just ahead, two spires reached skyward, two sentinels guarding a narrow pass. The pass reminded Vicky of the eye of a needle with the top sliced off.

"I certainly wouldn't want to thread that needle," Vicky thought with a slight shudder. That's why Kajar's next words shocked her like a jolt of electricity.

"Vicky," Kajar called back to her, "I'm going to sweep in as low as I can through the pass up ahead.

Fasten your eyes on the sides of the pass. Abdul-Bey has been known to camp out here."

Skillfully, Kajar maneuvered the small plane into the narrow corridor of the pass. The cliffs on either side of the plane were dangerously close to the plane's wing tips.

"Kajar, I see a white spot down there! Yes, yes. And it's surrounded by black spots. It could be Abdul-Bey's white tent!" Vicky cried.

Kajar gunned the plane through the pass and gained altitude as he swung out of it.

"We'll circle on the other side of the mountain and land," he said. "I want to give any ground observers the impression that I've continued on to the north," he explained.

He did just that, first losing himself in a cloud bank before he made the round-about maneuver and a skillful landing. Anyone watching from the ground would think he had gone on.

"We'll go the rest of the way on foot," Kajar announced as he killed the engine.

"But what do we do when we get there?" Ken Loring pointed out.

"Yes," Vicky put in. "Why won't they just take the three of us captive as they did before? I don't exactly relish the thought."

The three sat thinking. Silence filled the little plane.

"I think I've got it!" Vicky jumped up. The two men looked up at her vivid face.

"For the time being Kajar, you and Dad are going over to the enemy's side!"

# 14

## Desert Rescue

"THERE are just two things bothering me," Vicky said. "One, how can I fix myself up so *I* won't be recognized? And two, how can we be sure Skersh won't recognize Dad's famous face?"

"We can solve the first one easily," Kajar replied. "In the metal box over there, you will find things belonging to my sister, who sometimes travels with me in the plane. I am certain you will find a *chador* there."

"Good. But we just *can't* be sure of the other thing. Skersh has been about the world a good bit. I suspect he's been in America, too," Vicky said thoughtfully, remembering the dollar-sign money clip Yasmin had found at the remote dig. "How can we camouflage that handsome, world-wide face of yours, Dad?"

"I'm afraid," said Kajar, "there isn't much we can do about that. We'll just have to take a chance and hope no one recognizes him."

"Does this help?" Ken Loring asked, putting on dark glasses.

"It's amazing," said Vicky. It really *does* help. And if you don't talk at all, you may get away with it. Your voice would be a dead give-away. Let Kajar do all the talking—and interpret for you. It's a pretty big gamble, but it looks like the best we can do."

"Now that you've got the cast of characters, Miss Director, how about letting us in on the plot line of this story?" Ken Loring said, amusement coloring his voice.

"Well," Vicky began, "this is the general idea. Kajar's heard, we'll say, of the uprising plot. He'll tell Abdul-Bey he wants in on it. He'll pretend he wants to offer his Shiram-Zi men and his money. Dad, you'll be a top agent from the north country that's fomenting this whole thing. You're way over Skersh, and he can't do anything unless you give the O.K. And you're not ready to give the O.K. unless you see the oil exploration findings. While you're busy pow-wowing with Abdul, I'll get to Yasmin and Hakim and tell them to head for the plane. Skersh'll have to come with us to show us his oil findings at the remote dig. We'll have him cold, on the spot, with just the proof the Shah will need. You just have to be sure you get him to come with you."

"Kitten," Ken Loring said, "I can see holes in your plan, but it just might work. The thing to do is to take the offensive and move fast."

Kajar nodded his head. "Abdul-Bey is an easy man to fool. He would welcome any chance to be in league with the powerful Shiram-Zi. He will believe because he wants to believe."

With the arrangements made, the three set out. Vicky walked a few paces in back of the men as they came up to the sentry posted at the entrance of the camp.

Kajar and Ken Loring walked up to him belligerently. "I am Khan of Shiram-Zi, Kajar Mansur. Take me to Abdul-Bey."

The sentry hesitated. "Dog," Kajar shouted. "Be quick to it or I'll have your ears." The sentry started off toward the white tent. Ken Loring and Kajar were at his heels.

Vicky pretended at first to follow the men, but as soon as she could she sidled off and mixed with a group of women and children around a nearby campfire. Unobserved, she picked up a pottery bowl filled with some kind of grain and walked about with it, pretending to be busily preparing food.

Vicky walked from tent to tent, pounding the grain in the bowl. In the third tent she found herself staring into Yasmin's amber eyes.

"What do you want, woman?" Yasmin asked sharply. Her little face was streaked and dirty, as if she had been crying recently.

"Yasmin, where's Hakim? We haven't a minute to lose."

"Yasmin's hands fled to her mouth to stop the exclamation about to come out of it.

"Vicky?" she whispered. "Is it truly you?"

"Yes. Where's Hakim?" she repeated.

"He is out trying to find Skersh. He has not been in the captives' tent for two days. Hakim wonders what has become of him. We are frightened."

"Follow me outside," Vicky whispered. "Skirt the camp. If you spot Hakim, get him to follow me, too. I'll be at the campfire. Watch my every move."

Vicky went outside, still carrying the bowl of grain. She wandered to the fire and put the bowl down. She took a long stick and poked the fire vigorously, still unnoticed by the busy women of the tribe.

Soon she was aware that Yasmin and Hakim had joined her.

Without a sound, she picked up the bowl of grain again, moved away from the fire, and strolled toward the narrow open space where the sentry had again taken up his stand.

How to get past him? He would certainly recognize Hakim and would never let them pass. She had to think. She motioned Hakim and Yasmin to stop where they were.

Vicky scrambled up the rocky hill near the passageway and edged toward the guard. Hidden behind a jag of rock, she took a handful of the grain and showered it down on his head. She could see him look up, puzzled. She waited a moment and scattered another handful. The sentry stepped away from the opening and scratched his head. One more handful.

His curiosity overcame him. He started up the hill to investigate. Vicky slid down the other side of the hill, rolled behind a boulder, and watched the now unguarded opening.

She could have cheered as she saw Hakim and Yasmin scurry through it. She stood and waved them to her protected boulder.

The three of them huddled there until the sentry had finished his investigation. He sat down with a shrug. One of the women of the camp came up to him, carrying a dish.

"What luck!" Vicky whispered. "They've brought him his supper. We'll make a break for it when he starts to eat."

The guard took the dish from the woman's hand, lowered his head, and began to eat.

At Vicky's signal, the three headed for the hidden plane.

Once they were safely inside the plane, Vicky related her adventures from the time she had walked out of the camp with the nomad tribe. She told them what Kajar and her father were trying to accomplish with Abdul-Bey.

"But I wish they'd hurry back here," she said at last. "I want to get us all air-borne."

Her wish was granted.

"Here they come now!" Yasmin said excitedly. She pointed to the two men dog-trotting across the grassy plot toward the plane. "But only *two* men," Vicky exclaimed.

In moments, Kajar revved up the little craft, after making the group take special seats in the plane to distribute the load for take-off. Not until they were winging high in the sky did anyone try to talk.

"Dad, what happened in there? Where's Skersh? Why isn't he with you?" Vicky asked. "We *had* to have him with us."

"Skersh left the camp to rendezvous with a 'trusted comrade,' or so he told Abdul—a comrade who was bringing him maps of the oil find. Until he got those and dispatched them to his country, nothing could be done about the money for the revolution," Ken Loring answered.

"Did Abdul-Bey know where he was going for this meeting? Or who the 'trusted comrade' is?" Vicky questioned further.

"No, Skersh wouldn't take him into his confidence. Abdul's distrust of Skersh was beginning to show by the time we got there," Ken said.

"Yes," Kajar put in, "the whole atmosphere made things easier for us. It was easier to entice Abdul into our trap. Abdul-Bey is going to round up the wild-tribe chiefs and bring them to Shiram-Zi, supposedly for a conference. My men will hold them until I can return. We'll break this plot yet," Kajar said, pounding his knee with one fist.

"But Skersh! He'll get away," Vicky pointed out.

The whole group was silent, thinking over her words.

Vicky sat with her chin in her hand, puzzling. Her other hand, placed on her hip, strayed toward her pocket. She could feel a bulge there. The golden button. Her brain began to add up all the events from the Bagara bazaar on.

"Dad, Kajar," she said. "Let's go back to Reginald Wilson's dig. That's where we first met Skersh. That's where we might be able to pick up his trail. And, of course, that's where we'll find the proof we need."

Ken Loring looked long and hard at his daughter. "You're right, Vicky. It's the logical place to get a lead on Skersh. And once we have *him*, we may be able to trace the others involved in this plot."

"I've always wondered just what the tie-up is with Skersh and Pamela and Reginald Wilson," Vicky said, more to herself than to her father.

"The dig it is," Kajar agreed. "I'll see if I can radio Bagara and tell the Shah and Monsieur L-Hassa what has occurred so far." He busied himself with the transmitter.

Vicky looked around at Hakim and Yasmin as Kajar fiddled with the radio. They were both fast asleep, Yasmin's head nestled on Hakim's shoulder.

Vicky could see the excitement at the dig as the plane came in for a landing. The Zourabian workers waved their hands frantically. She could see two figures coming out of the main tent, a man and a woman. They shaded their eyes with their hands, looking up. Another man stood a little apart from them, fists clenched on his hips.

"Skersh!" Vicky exclaimed. Her father leaned over her shoulder to see the man—the man who had brought all this trouble to his daughter.

"I can hardly wait to get my hands on him," Ken Loring said between clenched teeth.

"No, Dad, no," Vicky protested. "Don't do anything —yet. Let's give him the rope and let him hang himself."

The people at the dig crowded around the door of the plane as Kajar, Ken Loring, and Vicky descended. Yasmin and Hakim were left asleep in the plane.

Reginald Wilson stepped forward. "Welcome once more to Kalpaz. I suppose you are here now on your official business, to photograph the dig." He smiled at Vicky. "You have come through your captivity unscathed, I see," he commented. "Yul has told us all about it—how he managed to get Yasmin and Hakim away from that savage, marauding tribe after you escaped. I was glad to hear you were all safe in Bagara."

Pamela Wilson stood surveying the scene quietly, her pale eyes staring out of her thin face. The jail had taken its toll.

Yul Skersh came forward and bowed low. "Once more we meet, Miss Loring. How nice to see you again. I trust you are well."

Inwardly, Vicky fumed. Skersh didn't know that she knew all about Hakim's and Yasmin's escape. For that matter, he didn't even know that she knew all about him and his evil plot. He had gotten away with a big lie once again—at least as far as Reginald Wilson was concerned. "Well," she thought to herself, "he won't get away with it much longer." She wanted to blurt out the whole truth right then and there. "Oooh," she thought angrily, "I can hardly wait to fix your wagon! And I will, Mr. Skersh, I will—just as soon as we have the proof."

Aloud, Vicky said, "Mr. Skersh, my father is most interested in the remote dig—*your* special little project." She underlined the last words. "Time is short. I wonder if you could take us there. Now!"

# 15

## Struggle in the Sand

"But of course," Skersh said surprisingly. "But I am afraid we shall have to go out there by horseback. You could never land your plane there," he added to Kajar.

Kajar began to sputter a reply. Vicky signaled him with her eyes, "Play along with him." Best to leave the plane here with Hakim and Yasmin still hidden there. Let Mister Skersh's "noble" tale of *his* rescue stand for now.

"Splendid," said Reginald Wilson. "I believe I'll join you this time, Skersh. About time I had a look at your discoveries out there."

"So!" Vicky thought. "Wilson hasn't seen the remote dig at all. Or he is lying through *his* teeth, too?"

Under Vicky's goading, the party lost no time in getting started.

As the others moved toward the horses, Kajar pulled Vicky aside. "I'll fly Yasmin and Hakim to Bagara. And while I'm there, I'll see the Shah and Monsieur L-Hassa in person and tell them we have located Skersh here. They will send help."

"Good, Kajar," Vicky said. "Skersh is slippery, as you can see. But the proof is at the remote dig—and I'll show him up—somehow.

"Oh," Vicky went on, "I almost forgot. Here is your ring, your ring of allegiance to the Shah." She stretched it toward him, the blue-green stones glinting in the sunlight.

Kajar smiled. "Since I go myself to swear allegiance, I do not need the ring to symbolize my loyalty. Keep it, little one. As a true daughter of the Shiram-Zi, you are entitled to it. As the one who helped save my country, you are doubly entitled to wear it. Go, fair friend, and . . . take care," Kajar added softly.

As Vicky watched him stride away toward the plane, her thoughts were far away from the desert—at a table at the Orly air terminal. Jeff Hubbell had used those very words.

Pamela Wilson insisted on going with them to the remote dig in spite of her husband's protests, and in the end she had her way.

"You have not been well since that unfortunate incident in Bagara. You should have followed Monsieur L-Hassa's advice on your release and gone to a hospital for rest," Reginald Wilson said.

"No, no. I *must* be with you."

Vicky caught the note of frenzy in Pamela's voice, and wondered at the woman's insistence.

The ride out to the dig was uneventful. Vicky urged everyone on. She was the first to pull up her horse as they reached the spot.

She dashed from her horse to the tent Skersh had said was his. She wrenched the flap back and entered. The blanket which had hung at the back of the tent was gone! She found herself staring at blank, smooth canvas.

The seismograph and the wire and the crates and batteries had completely disappeared!

While the group watched her frantic pace in amazement, Vicky zipped outside and over to the place where she had seen the drills. Nothing! Everything had been removed.

She wheeled about and saw Skersh, his face broadened with a triumphant smirk.

"Ah," he said smoothly. "Such excitement. I did not know the dig held so much interest for you."

"Dad!" Vicky cried. "It's gone! The equipment . . . the instruments . . . all the proof that Skersh was here trying to discover oil! And he did discover it, I know he did. But the evidence . . ." her voice trailed off. She was close to tears. "It's gone, Dad. There's nothing here."

"Oil?" Reginald Wilson sputtered. "Impossible! Yul Skersh is an archeologist, a good one. He knows nothing of the science of oil exploration."

"The girl is obviously mistaken," Skersh said to the group. To Ken Loring he explained kindly, "Her captivity must have been too arduous for her. There has never been anything here except my few excavation tools, these few tents for workmen. She is mistaken."

"Why, you . . .you," Ken stepped forward, his fists clenched. He stopped himself just in time.

"Look in the excavation!" Vicky cried. "Mr. Wilson, see if anything is buried there."

Reginald Wilson shook his head as if to say "poor thing." He walked over to the hole covered with tarpaulin. He flung it back and knelt to peer in. He came back to the group.

"Nothing. The usual cuts—all done with a spade," he announced.

Vicky strode up and down in desperation. The incriminating evidence was gone. What could she *do* without the proof she had expected to find? She whacked her sides. Her hand struck the button in her pocket.

She wrenched it from her pocket. The desert breeze picked up the tissue it had been wrapped in and whisked it away. The golden button flashed.

"And what about this button, Mr. Skersh?" Vicky called wildly. "What about *this button?*"

Skersh lunged toward her. Vicky backed away from him, holding the button tightly clenched in her fist.

Ken Loring and Reginald Wilson grabbed at Skersh and missed.

Vicky stumbled in the soft sand. Skersh clutched at her. Wild-eyed, he tried to claw her hand open.

Vicky saw him suddenly wrenched backward, heard the crack as Ken Loring's fist smashed into Skersh's jaw. Yul Skersh toppled over in the sand.

Vicky sat panting, her eyes darting about her.

"Someone see to Pamela," she said wearily. "She's fainted."

# 16

## Bursting Baubles

VICKY turned the button over and over in her hand.

"After all, it's only a button. Why were you so anxious to have it, Mr. Skersh?" Vicky said to the still-unconscious man. "Why?"

Vicky brought the golden shape closer to her eyes, examining it. A jagged seam, no more than a thread, wound its way in and out of the delicate and intricate carvings on the button. She pressed it with her fingers. Nothing happened.

She took the button by the little "eye" which once had held it fastened to Pamela Wilson's chador-coat. She twiddled it back and forth. It gave out a tiny

163

click as she twirled it. Vicky was reminded of the click a combination lock made.

"That's it! A combination of some kind, some sort of tiny locking device. Najeeb said the Zourabian jewelsmiths were masters at their trade. *That Najeeb!*" The name she shouted aloud seemed to propel her from her place on the sand.

Still clutching the button, she ran over to Pamela Wilson who was being brought out of her faint by Reginald and Ken Loring.

"Najeeb," the woman murmured softly, like a faint echo of Vicky's own voice.

A moan from Skersh alerted Ken Loring. "Keep an eye on him, Reginald, while I find something to tie him with."

"The tent ropes, Dad, they'll do," Vicky suggested. "Here, I'll take care of Pamela. You see to him over there."

"Najeeb," Pamela mumbled again. "I don't know where . . . button . . . is . . . where any buttons . . . are." The words came out jerkily as the woman twisted in Vicky's arms. She seemed to be reliving, in her dream state, something that had happened to her. Her face contorted as if she were in pain.

Gently, Vicky smoothed the woman's pale hair, trying to comfort her.

"Hurry, Dad," she called out. "We'd better get Pamela back to the Wilson dig. She doesn't seem to be coming out of this at all."

The two men lashed the now-conscious Skersh on his horse. The man's eyes were bleary and sullen. He said nothing at all, but his arms strained against the ropes which held him.

Reginald Wilson and Ken Loring rigged a drag sled from the camp cot in Skersh's tent for the unconscious Pamela. They attached it to her horse.

It would be slow going back to the first dig, Vicky knew. The mystery of the golden button would have to wait until then.

The bizarre band started off. They hadn't gone more than a mile when a cloud of sand in the distance announced the arrival of help.

"It's the Shah's men," Vicky explained. "Kajar said he would get them out here to help us."

A jeep, its wheels tracked for fast movement over the sand, met the group. Behind the wheel was Najeeb. But he was entirely alone. None of the Shah's men were with him.

Vicky turned to Skersh. His eyes glinted now. A wise smile flickered on, then quickly off.

Najeeb was out of the jeep in a flash. "I have orders to take this man directly into Bagara," he said imperiously, pointing to Skersh. The beads on his headdress flashed like lightning as he moved closer and tried to take Skersh's arm.

"No! No!" Vicky protested.

"Why not?" Ken Loring asked his daughter. "Surely he can be trusted with L-Hassa's secretary."

"But there's something between them. I know it. He had one of Pamela's buttons on his desk. I saw it there. And Pamela has been muttering his name in a strange way. If we turn Skersh over to Najeeb, Skersh will get away, I know it!" Vicky begged. "Wait, please wait for the others."

"The girl talks nonsense," Najeeb said. "There will be no others. I have been sent here to take him into custody."

Ken Loring looked first at Najeeb and then at his daughter. He frowned. "I'll go along with you, Vicky. But I hope you're right. If you are wrong, if Najeeb is on the up-and-up . . . you'll have some tall explaining to do."

"Please, give me a little time. Keep Skersh tied. Let's all get into the jeep and get Pamela back where we can fix her up. She knows something, I'm sure. Please." There was desperation in Vicky's voice.

Reginald Wilson came up at Vicky's outburst. "Mr. Loring, I think your daughter is right. Pamela has not been herself since she returned to the dig. She jumps at the mention of Najeeb's name. Something has terrified her. I'd like to get to the bottom of it."

Najeeb started quickly to climb into the jeep. Too quickly.

"Just a moment," Ken Loring said sharply. "I'll do the driving."

Najeeb stopped and turned frantically toward Skersh. Vicky was positive she saw Skersh nod his head just a fraction. Najeeb flung himself sullenly into the back seat.

Reginald hustled Skersh into the back seat beside him. Then he lifted his wife and seated her carefully on the front seat.

"You sit with her," he said to Vicky. "I'll see to these two in back."

The jeep roared away toward the Kalpaz dig.


"Put her here," Vicky ordered. "And where's your first-aid kit, Mr. Wilson?"

Gently, the men put the unconscious woman on the cot. She moaned. "No button . . . no button." Her eyelids fluttered and then opened wide. Vicky soothed her.

"Don't try to say anything just yet," she cautioned. "You should rest first."

But Pamela's eyes lighted on Najeeb, seated in one corner of the tent, guarded by Ken Loring. She started up in fright.

"It's all right, Pam dear," Reginald said, "he can't hurt you."

Pamela sank back. She put a hand weakly to her forehead. "He was horrid in Bagara. Najeeb. Each day he came to my cell and questioned me for hours on hours about a button off my coat. He would not let me eat or sit or have water to drink. Hour after hour. I did not know about the buttons. All I knew was that they were gone."

"Why did he finally let you go?" Vicky asked.

"Monsieur L-Hassa himself came to the jail and saw that I was released. He wanted me to go to a hospital or to his home, but I refused. I had to get back to Reginald."

"Why didn't you tell Monsieur L-Hassa of Najeeb's cruelty?" Vicky queried.

"He . . . Najeeb told me that if I ever breathed a word of it to anyone he would have Reginald arrested as a spy. He said he could convince the Shah and British officials, too, that Reginald was spying for a foreign power. He said he had proof. He said it would mean death under Zourabian law. I was terrified for Reginald."

"Did he ever say why you were arrested in the bazaar that time in Bagara?"

Najeeb jumped up, his mustache quivering. Ken Loring pushed him back roughly.

"No," Pamela answered weakly, still watching Najeeb. "I was never told anything about why I was taken or held. And I could not understand why Reginald never came to Bagara to get me."

"I would have, my dear. Oh, I would have," Reginald said, kneeling at his wife's side. "But Yasmin L-Hassa and Vicky said you were to be released, that it was all a mistake. When you didn't appear, I talked to Najeeb. He told me I must tread carefully with Zourabian authorities. If I made a fuss they would cancel the dig and expel us both from Zourab. Foolishly, selfishly, I believed him. He convinced me that everything was all right and that you were well and happy. And when I spoke to the people at the consulate, they told me you had been released."

"It's all right, all right," Pamela stroked her husband's hand. "But why did he want the button from my coat? They were just . . . buttons." Her voice trailed off. She closed her eyes. Even, peaceful breaths arose from her lips.

"She's asleep," Vicky announced after inspecting her. "She'll be fine after she's rested."

Vicky stood up and pulled the golden button from her pocket. She thrust it under Najeeb's nose. Skersh squirmed against the ropes that held him.

Najeeb started to reach out his hand toward Vicky. Ken Loring slapped it away.

"I've had it all along," she said. "I found it in the bazaar. I never returned it to Pamela. She never knew I had it."

Vicky turned to her father. "Fish in his pockets, Dad. See if you can find the ones that match it. I think Najeeb is the 'trusted comrade' Skersh was going to meet at the dig, and I have a pretty strong suspicion that the buttons are the key to the proof we need."

Ken Loring dragged Najeeb to his feet. He hung like a limp doll as Reginald Wilson and Ken held him.

The contents of his pockets were spilled out and tossed on the table. There were no buttons, just a few coins and the gold disc Najeeb had showed her in place of the button she had spotted on his desk.

With sudden inspiration, Vicky snatched off the headdress Najeeb wore. She fumbled in its folds. One, two, three golden buttons lay in her hand.

"Give me the combination. Tell me the trick," she demanded.

Najeeb looked up at her scornfully and said nothing. His eyes slipped to the table.

Vicky snatched up the gold disc. She clicked open the circular letter opener and the blade uncurled. She pressed the delicate point against the fastening of the button with deliberate care. The bauble burst open like a ripe seed pod.

Vicky extracted the thin piece of paper folded inside. She applied the knife point to each button in succession. They each held a paper.

Quickly she smoothed them out on the table before her.

"Maps! Each one contains a map!" she cried triumphantly.

The sudden sound of an engine outside froze the whole group motionless. Brakes squealed and brisk commands sounded, followed by the thud of boots on sand. Monsieur L-Hassa, flanked by two giant policemen in the peacock-blue uniform of the Shah's palace guard, stood in the doorway of the tent. The Chief Counsel's face was a thunderstorm of rage.

Ken Loring pushed his charges toward the burly, uniformed men.

"They're yours. Take them away," he said. "Vicky has the evidence right here."

Monsieur L-Hassa came to the table where Vicky had turned her attention. She handed him the slips of paper.

"I never could read maps very well," she said. "Like most women, I guess. But I think you'll find these are north, south, east, and west elevation maps of the oil field Skersh found."

Monsieur L-Hassa scanned the papers rapidly. "You read maps very well, my dear," he said.

Vicky slumped into a camp chair nearby. "You know what I need right now?" she stated. "A big fluffy, hot bath."

# 17

# Kajar Comes Through

THE official car, with M. L-Hassa, the prisoners and guards, drove off in the lead.

"I shall take no chances with my traitorous Najeeb," M. L-Hassa had sighed deeply. "His father was long the trusted right hand of my father who preceeded me as Chief Counsel. I overlooked his pompous manners, his stupid little poses. I forgave him too much in the name of his father."

In the second jeep, Reginald and a restored Pamela bounced merrily in the back while Vicky sat with her father in the front.

"Pam, can you think back to that very first day at

the jail?" Vicky asked over her shoulder. "Why did your whole manner change so suddenly? You were so relaxed at first, and then you seemed frightened."

"I saw a face at the window," Pamela answered. "I was suddenly struck with the awfulness of my situation. I guess I panicked."

"I saw the face too. I'd been followed by the same man on my way back from the bazaar," Vicky admitted.

"You were *what!*" Ken Loring exploded. "Why didn't you tell me?"

"The same reason why you haven't told me about that letter the Zourabian gave you at Orly," Vicky said, her nose in the air.

Ken was silent for a moment. "The letter warned me not to photograph the dig at Kalpaz. It said some mumbo-jumbo about disturbing the gods and the souls of the ancients haunting me and my daughter to our dying day."

Vicky laughed. "Dad, I'm surprised at you! Surely you didn't let any hocus-pocus like that scare you! You couldn't have believed it!"

"Not for myself, but I didn't like that mention of 'my daughter.' We were on our way to a strange and mysterious place. I didn't want anything happening to you."

"Was the letter signed?" Vicky asked.

"No. But I see now that it must have come from Yul Skersh."

"Then the letter was what made you hesitate about letting me go on that trip to the dig with Hakim and Yasmin."

"Yes," Ken Loring answered. "I was torn about that trip to the dig. I didn't want you to go, and then I did. I thought maybe that inquisitive little nose of yours might smell out something." Ken tweaked the nose he'd mentioned. "I thought Hakim and Yasmin would be safe enough bodyguards for you. It turned out just the opposite, of course."

"Since this seems to be the day for true confessions, *mon cher père*, I'll let you in on something else. My room at the hotel was ransacked when I got back to Bagara after my *jalboot* trip," Vicky said.

"Ransacked? Why?"

"I'll never be sure, of course, but I think someone must have been after the button. Nothing was taken. Anyhow, in the middle of the shambles, I began to think awfully, awfully hard about the importance of that gold button."

Pamela and Reginald had been silent during the whole conversation. Now Pamela leaned forward with interest.

"But Najeeb thought *I* had the fourth button. That's why he kept after me. He asked me about my coat buttons so often I thought I would lose my mind. I never did understand why he was so interested in them."

The whole group in the jeep was silent and thoughtful for a while.

"The face at the window!" Vicky said suddenly. "That man must have thought I gave you the button, and reported it to Najeeb. When he couldn't break you down, he must have had my room searched in a last desperate try to uncover it."

"I think you've got something there, kitten," Ken Loring said.

"I say," Reginald broke in. "Wherever did you have it hidden?"

"I stuck it in my jar of cold cream. And I'll never know why I did it, except . . ."

"Except what?" Ken Loring asked. His admiration for Vicky's ingenuity showed clearly on his face.

"Except that's where Aunt Ellen always used to hide her rings when she was in a strange hotel. I must have been thinking of her at the time. I hope she'll be pleased," Vicky added with an affectionate little laugh.

Reginald's nasal laugh sounded. "Oh, you clever Americans," he said.

Vicky virtually flew to her room once the jeep had stopped at the hotel. As she opened the door, she caught the whiff of a subtle, marvelous perfume.

Yasmin jumped up from the cushions where she had been seated. The little ragamuffin who had been left sleeping in Kajar Mansur's plane had been transformed once again into a golden doll. She was dressed in a silk dress the color of her amber eyes, and wore a gold *zada* over her head.

"Hi," she caroled. "Long time no look!"

Vicky collapsed, laughing, in a chair. "Long time no see, Yasmin."

Yasmin clapped her hands smartly together and two servants came to her side. "Your bath is ready, Vicky," she said. "Help her out of those icky clothes," she ordered the two women.


Vicky's suspicion about the ransacking of her room was right.

At dinner that night at the L-Hassas' sumptuous home, Monsieur L-Hassa told her that the authorities had gotten a full confession from Najeeb about his traitorous activities.

"Each week when Pamela Wilson came into town, she unknowingly carried messages from Skersh to Najeeb in the buttons of her *chador*. Usually, they were just orders. The detail maps of the oil field were to be taken on Mrs. Wilson's last, unfortunate shopping trip. Najeeb was to send them across the border to the north while Skersh rallied the wild tribes for action."

"What prevented his removing the maps from the buttons as he had removed the other messages?" Vicky asked.

"Mrs. Wilson did not take tea with him as she had done on every other trip. He got anxious and had her arrested so he could take the buttons. He knew that he could always say the arrest was an error—and he planned to. But you can well imagine his panic when the fourth button—with the key map in it—could not be found. One of the spies in his pay saw you pick up something in the bazaar. He reported it to Najeeb, and he also reported that he thought you had given it to Pamela at the jail."

"And the kidnapping of Yasmin and Hakim and me, then," Vicky reasoned, "was just so Skersh could have an ace up his sleeve until the fourth button was found."

"Right," Monsieur L-Hassa said.

"And Kajar Mansur? Have you heard from him?" Vicky asked.

"Indeed. The wild-tribe chieftains were taken and held by his men. Kajar has convinced them of how they were duped by Skersh and how he would have—what do you say—double-crossed them. He succeeded in convincing two of them so strongly that they have come to swear allegiance to the Shah after these many years."

"And Abdul-Bey?"

"He remains wild and free as ever, but chastened. He has lost face with his tribe. He will do no damage," Monsieur L-Hassa ended.

# 18

## VIP Vicky

"DON'T forget to write me!" Yasmin called to Vicky as Ken and his daughter headed for the small plane that would take them out of Zourab.

Vicky shifted the saddlebag Hakim had given her from one hand to the other. She waved her arm. The Shiram-Zi carpet she carried over it fluttered in the breeze. Kajar's ring twinkled on her hand.

"I won't forget," she promised.

The two of them stood briefly, waving back at each other.

"Wasn't Yasmin something, Dad?" she said.

"She certainly was," her father agreed.

"Whoosh." Vicky plopped down on the seat when they had boarded the plane. "We have really been at it in the last days, haven't we *just!*"

The trials of Najeeb and Skersh had been swift ones, all thoroughly covered by Ken Loring and Vicky for the documentary. The Zourab story was being told around the world. Her father would have the only fully photographed tale of this fascinating little country, now more than ever in the world's eye.

"You know," she said. "I think I'm going to like your interview with El Mohama Shah-ja the best of all. The whole thing is brilliant, just brilliant."

"You're pretty shining yourself, kitten. If it hadn't been for you, the documentary might be just another travelogue of the smallest country in existence. You've really given it punch."

"Huh," Vicky said. "Be off with you and your fancy compliments. And let me get some 'closed eye' until we change to the jet at Zurich."

"All right, all right, fellas. Let them through. Let them through. *Donnez les passages!*"

Jeff Hubbell! That awful French! It had to be none other. Vicky glowed at the sound of his voice. She never realized she'd be so delighted to hear it, terrible accent and all.

Airport officials, camera men, reporters buzzed like hornets about Vicky and her father at the Orly airport where they had just touched down.

The man who seemed to be in charge of the whole buzz fought his way to Ken Loring. "You may interview them in the lounge. You may interview them in the lounge," he kept saying as he elbowed his way to Ken's side.

"A thousand pardons," he said to Ken in French. "I didn't know if you wanted it or not. But they would not be put off. We've had to set up a press conference for you. We trust it is all right."

"Certainly," Ken Loring said. "That will be perfectly all right."

The official ran interference for Kenneth Loring. Vicky kept behind her father's broad back. The mass of people pushed through the doors into the lobby.

"Where's Jeff?" Vicky kept wondering. "I just *know* that was his voice I heard."

The official helped Vicky up two steps to a small platform where microphones stood on a table. He seated her before one and adjusted the mike for her. He leaned over her shoulder and announced that the press conference was open for questions.

"Mr. Loring," a voice with a French accent said, "how did you first find out about the conspiracy."

Ken Loring rose. "Just a moment," he said to the whole group. "The story is really not mine to tell. It is my daughter's. May I present her, gentlemen of the press? Victoria Loring."

"Oh, no, Dad," Vicky said in a low voice. "I'll never be able to handle all the questions by myself. I don't want . . ."

"I'll let you see how it feels to be on the receiving instead of the asking end," Ken whispered back. "Just take a deep breath and plunge in." He pulled her to her feet.

Flashlight bulbs began to pop like small bubbles around her. She looked out at the sea of upraised faces, hunting for that one familiar one.

The questions, in several different accents, but all in English, were thrown at her.

When did she discover the conspiracy? . . . How did she figure out the secret of the buttons? . . . Just how did she escape from the wild-tribe encampment? . . . What does the dig at Kalpaz look like? . . . Is the Shah's palace as ornate as she expected? . . . Describe Yasmin, please.

"Who is this Kajar Mansur?" one voice bellowed over the crowd. It was unmistakably Jeff Hubbell's.

Vicky paused and peered at her audience. She saw his blond crew cut sticking up over most of the reporters' heads. His blue eyes looked into hers from the distance.

Vicky paused and took a deep breath. The crowd hushed.

"Well," she began. She purposely let her voice gush, just a little. "He's just about the handsomest man I've ever seen. Tall, tanned, and terrific just about sums him up. He's young, but very intelligent, very mature. He is one of the most powerful men in Zourab, a Khan —that means chief, you know," she over-explained, not being able to resist needling Jeff a bit. "He's Khan of all the Shiram-Zi, one of the Shah's most trusted tribes. It was he who saved my life in the desert when I escaped from the wild tribe." She stopped to let her last words sink into Jeff's ears.

The other reporters, sparked by Jeff's question and her answer, pressed her for more details about the Khan.

Vicky looked straight at Jeff as she answered. Was he fuming? She couldn't tell. He was making notes and his head was down.

She raised the carpet she had carried into the airport lounge with her, showing it to the reporters to explain a point.

"I was officially adopted into the Shiram-Zi. I am considered a true daughter. This is my home," she went on, raising the carpet higher. A cameraman caught the pose. "They have a saying, 'Where my carpet is, there is my home.' I shall always consider this a treasured possession." Vicky sat down.

"Thank you, Miss Loring," Jeff's voice boomed out, ending the interview in the presidential press conference manner.

The reporters left. Jeff still stood at the back of the room where he had been during the interview. He sauntered over to her when the space in front of the platform was cleared.

He leaned his elbows on the table and looked up at her.

"And now, Miss Loring, how about the *real* story? For instance, where did you get that big fat ring?"